Sound of a Murder

Original Manuscript in Norwegian by:

Pål Undall

Translated and adapted to English by:

Kim Wingerei

Sound of a Murder

First Published in Norway in 2017 by Publica Bok AS, Oslo, Norway

NATIONAL
LIBRARY
OF AUSTRALIA

A catalogue record for this book is available from the National Library of Australia

ISBN: 978-0-6482638-0-7 (paperback)
ISBN: 978-0-6482638-1-4 (e-book)

Published by Kim Wingerei
www.kimwingerei.com

With special thanks to Pål Undall, for his generosity,
to Dixie Isobel for grammar and fact checking,
to Renée Otmar for her sage advice on all things writing,
and finally Fiona Jones at Author Express for her patient
support and endless enthusiasm!

More than the eye can see

The paddle gave away a gentle splashing sound every time it left the surface, the canoe gliding silently through the water, the bow twisting and rising for every stroke. Not a breath of wind, not a cloud in the sky, eerily quiet.

I lifted the paddle and put it in my lap, lent forward, grasped the bow seat with both hands and yelled out at the very top of my voice: "FAAARK!" The sound rolled across the water like thunder before disappearing into the densely forested hills that surrounded the lake.

I grabbed the paddle and kept going, that physical outpouring did help to relieve some of the tension. I was aiming for a small island towards the north end of the lake. I had found the lake earlier as I searched Google Maps at random, starting in Oslo, clicked the direction arrow a few times and zoomed in. The canoe belonged to a good mate, he wouldn't even know it was missing by the time he got it back. The camping gear was my own. I had food and drink for a few days, the mobile was turned off, the SIM-card was in my back pocket as an extra precaution.

Google Maps indicated that the lake was rather remote, but it turned out not quite to be the case. Holiday houses of various sizes lined the shore, mostly the typical modest log cabins so common throughout Norway, but also a few modern ones with over-sized terraces and satellite antennas on the roof. I wondered vaguely at why someone would invest in a holiday house here rather than on the sea shore or in the mountains, but each to their own. Lucky for me, this time of year they were all empty, made ready for winter, outdoor furniture well covered and dinghies turned upside down in preparation for the snow. The only signs of life were the screeches of a couple of crane birds on a rocky outcrop nearby, and the odd rifle shot in the distance; the moose hunting season was still on.

The little island started to take form beneath the hills in the background. Tall pine trees foreboding at first, then revealing an idyllic little beach as I got closer. Tempting, but too open, even though I didn't really think anyone would find me here. I paddled around the island and found two more camping spots, selecting the one furthest from the shore.

Dragging the canoe behind some shrubs and out of sight, I started unpacking. The tent was given to me by an uncle on my 14th birthday, no doubt with the underlying hope that I would develop healthy interests in life. For every Christmas thereafter he gave me more gear, a sleeping bag, a swag, a gas cooker, a backpack, as well as books on how to survive outdoors. I never thought I'd get to use any of it, but here I was, alone in the wilderness, needing to survive without modern amenities for a few days. I sent my uncle thoughts of long overdue gratitude.

Never used, the tent was still in its original packaging, with a user guide which of course I ignored. With usual self-belief I winged it, surrendering only after having broken a tent pole and ripped a seam, finally scanning the manual enough to erect the tent within a few minutes. I was tempted to just lie down there and then, not having had any sleep for a couple of days, but decided instead to survey my temporary island hide-away. In the little inlet someone had decorated a small fir-tree with beer cans and a couple of used condoms, a bit like a Christmas tree. An idea I thought to adopt if I was going to enjoy another Christmas eve. In the other camping spot that I had seen earlier, there was a neat stack of dried logs for a fire, and I thought they'd come in handy to keep me warm during the night.

Even though I had brought both beer and a bottle of Jack Daniels, I had a real craving for coffee. I had used my little gas cooker many times during my student days while living in shared lodgings without access to a kitchen. Soon the smell of coffee filled my nostrils and I took my swag, the sleeping bag and the whiskey to a comfortable spot right by the lake shore. The sun was starting to cast long shadows, I poured a wee dram in my coffee and felt the warm liquid run down my throat, soothing and calming. I let the feeling linger.

I was soon drawn to the sight of a birch tree by the water's edge, thinking how this time of year, without leaves, peering through the branches you wouldn't necessarily know if it was spring or autumn - if the days were getting longer or shorter. Only the few brown leaves floating away like large birthmarks on top of the water revealed the inevitable proximity of winter. Along the rocks that formed the shore were gnarly exposed roots clinging onto what little soil was there. I looked up at the old fir-tree, hundreds of years old. It had been there during good times and bad, seen war and famine, unperturbed by it all. I looked down at my own sweaty hands, rubbed them against my jeans, took another sip of the whiskey. Like my ancestors before me, I picked up a stick and started drawing lines in the sand, drew figures of old mammoths and over-sized moose in epic fights with hunters using long spears. I was immersed in my little fantasy world when reality hit me like an icy dagger.

The distinctive sound of an outboard engine starting. I could see an old fashioned wooden dinghy coming towards me from across the lake, thankfully at an angle towards the rear of the island, one man at the tiller, still unable to see me in the shadows of the trees. I quickly gathered my stuff and scampered back to my tent. Was it one of Aron's men? It was possible, but I couldn't work out how. The only possible trace could have been my Google search sitting at an Internet cafe downtown Oslo. If they knew I was there, they would have gotten to me there! To be safe, I pulled the centre pole of the tent and flattened it. I could hear the high pitched sound of the small outboard approaching.

What to do if they found me? I had a knife and a small axe, but against the big, burly thug who chased me down the street yesterday, I wouldn't stand a chance. Was that him in the dinghy? The island was large enough so I could hide for a while, but then what? He could just take the canoe and my gear, call for reinforcements, wait it out.

The sound of the engine got louder, I took the knife and the axe and moved deeper in between the trees, towards the inlet on the other side. As I knelt down, I could see a man standing up in the boat, coming straight towards where I was. It certainly wasn't the one that chased me. He was bald and clean-shaven, whereas this guy had a beard and a full head of hair. It could still be another one of Aron's henchmen, of course, but as I anxiously considered this, he proceeded to circumnavigate the island and returned to where he came from. The sun was setting behind the tall, majestic trees on the top of the ridge to the west, in half an hour it would be dark.

So for now I would have to stay where I was. Maybe I should leave the island under the cover of darkness? To be on the safe side I let the tent be and took the gas cooker and some food and drinks with me into the forest glen. I heated up a couple of chicken legs, drank a lukewarm beer. A couple of times I could see beams of light coming from cars driving towards the spot the man in the boat had come from. Soon I could see lights from a cabin and I realised that he was probably just a man visiting his holiday house, having invited a few guests. Quite a relief, but still something didn't feel quite right, there was a reason he had done the trip out to the island, as if to check that there was nobody there. Why? I decided to stay undetected for now.

With my coffee, whiskey, swag and sleeping bag I sat down by the water again. The sun had gone, and with that the warmth, but the moon was up, and the stars as bright as they can only be this far away from city lights. There was no wind. Another set of light beams swept over the water pane as a third car arrived at the cabin. Suddenly it came to life over there, and even though it was at least 500 metres away from where I sat I could hear a lot of what was said, as if they were a mere stone's throw away. It's a well known phenomenon, sounds carry extremely well over the water, but to experience it myself was almost spooky. Another car arrived and was received with much enthusiasm by those already there. Then it went quiet, they must all have retreated to the cabin. Whatever was going on over there had nothing to do with me.

I remained sitting by the water for a while, some big swigs of the whiskey, starting to doze off. But soon after I had to get out of my sleeping bag for a piss, and at the same time I could again hear activity from the area of the cabin. A large bonfire was now burning, flames stretching up towards the stars and brilliantly reflecting in the clear and still lake. It was beautiful. In amongst the sparkling sounds of the fire I could still hear voices. Gunnar, Joe and Kai were names uttered. I could only hear one female voice, her name was Vivian. They were talking about a boating holiday, rowdy drinking trips to Sweden, logging, wolves and catching yabbies, all common enough topics of conversation around these parts. Spirits seemed to be soaring around the bonfire as the evening went by, with much laughter and loud hilarity. I contemplated paddling across to join the party; a stranger in a canoe would be warmly welcomed I thought. But I was too comfortable where I was, half drunk, peering up at the magnificent night sky.

Which is why I wasn't paying attention when the mood changed across the lake. But the tone had turned from frivolous and light hearted to confrontational and argumentative. "Damn you, Steve, play on the same team for a change", "you are so fucking stubborn", "I can't" and "go fuck yourself". It was obvious that the one called Steve was on the defensive. I was lying there waiting on the next salvo, maybe even the sounds of fisticuffs, but instead it suddenly went quiet. All I could hear was the crackling sound of the dying fire. I figured that they must have come to their senses, turned in for the night. Just as I was about to do the same, the silence was broken by a sharp, very loud bang. It took me a second or two to realise what I had just heard, but all doubt disappeared with the piercing shriek from the woman, slicing through the cool, clear night.

Aron

"Carl, get the boys", Aron barked down to the restaurant below. Thirty years and 100 kilos ago Aron had been the Norwegian weightlifting champion. Today a web search would find him as the owner and manager of Torpedo Pizza, boasting the fastest pizza delivery service in Oslo. Even though both the police and the taxation department were quite aware of his actual activities, and more than annoyed at the blatant arrogance of the man, he covered his tracks so well that they just couldn't get anything on him that would ever hold up in court.

Carl, Thor and Vladimir marched up the stairs a bit like sheep to the slaughter. Tired and discouraged after a day and a night searching without results. Vladimir stooped by the window, his eyes repeatedly peering into the backyard displaying his usual paranoia, whilst Carl and Thor slouched down on the leather couch. Aron sat back into his specially reinforced recliner chair, a scornful smirk as he folded his arms across his rather intimidating ribcage. "Well if it isn't Santa Claus and his little helpers? A bit too early with the presents this year, were we?" The question festering in the air for a few moments, Aron's unpredictability too well known. He could explode at a mere trifle, inflict serious injury on someone without apparent reason, at other times he could be both magnanimous and forgiving. Hence neither of the three men dared speak or meet Aron's gaze, staring into the ground like errant kids.

Carl just wanted to beat the living daylight out of somebody, anybody, but he knew that he would have to take the brunt of the blame. "The problem", he finally ventured as he spread his arms out as an Italian soccer player pleading innocence, "the problem was that he must have recognised me from when he came here and picked up the cash. We passed each other in the hallway as he entered and I was on my way out." Carl swallowed as little beads of sweat appeared on his bald head before continuing. "It was Friday afternoon when Thor got a tip-off from someone having seen Marius on the street. We were there in ten minutes, no more, the tipster had followed him and pointed him out just as the bastard turned around, looking right at me. He spun around like a fuckin' weasel, I ran straight for him, pushing people aside and almost got to him before he vanished into thin air. Just like that, he was gone, had me totally confused. There were five of us and two cars, he was surrounded but still he managed to get away, and stay away. Fucked if I know, we went into every shop in the street, searched every toilet, office, storeroom and fitting room. We even got anyone parked in the area to open their trunks. We looked fuckin' everywhere, but the little shithead was gone." Carl shook his head in exasperation, not quite knowing what the reaction would be.

But instead of another sarcastic comment, an angry outburst or another question, Aron started cracking his knuckles, one at the time, each one slowly, audibly. Thor, nicknamed The Hammer for several reasons, couldn't stand it, the sound was like chalk on chalkboard to him, and Aron knew it all too well. As if on cue, Thor blurted out: "That was it Aron, just like that, honest to God, he just vanished like a fucking wizard. But don't worry, we'll find him. All the boys have his picture on their mobiles and Barry has broken into his apartment and is there waiting for him should he decide to come home. We've got people everywhere round-the-clock, the train station, docklands, the harbour, fucking everywhere! And I've got my mate at the phone company on alert to call me as soon as they can trace his mobile. It'll be OK, Aron, just relax."

Asking Aron to relax was normally like a red rag to a bull, and both Vladimir and Carl looked anxiously at Thor as they steeled themselves for the inevitable explosion. But glancing at Aron, still sitting in the same position with his arms crossed, they saw a slight smile forming on his face: "OK then, suppose it's all fine then, I can just relax, all good, mate." Pausing for a second or two he continued evenly: "But just in case, and only if you have the time, maybe you should look into this Marius Tokle a bit closer. Maybe find out about his family, his friends, girlfriend and where he works. Does he have any vices, maybe an old auntie he visits regularly? Because if he either hasn't paid me, or we haven't found him within three weeks, someone in this room will pay the price!".

Except for the humming of the ceiling fan, the silence was deafening. Nobody moved a finger or dared shift their gaze. At long last Aron lifted his right bear claw of a hand as if waving away a fly: "OK lads, you can go. Get to work."

~ ~ ~

What the hell, what just happened? Somebody had been shot over there! I crawled down to the water's edge and listened intensely. One of them shouting: "Gunnar, what the fuck?" Someone sobbed. Another tried whispering, without success: "Shut up, for God's sake, somebody might be listening!" My heart racing I crouched down even further. "Fuck, fuck, fuck, what do we do now?" "Gunnar, you're fuckin' crazy, he's dead!"

I should have stayed there listening, but I was too scared. If it wasn't already bad enough, now I was a witness to a murder as well. I kind of lost it for a while, just sat there staring at the water in total apathy, not caring about anything anymore. And I was drunk.

I don't know how long I sat there, but it was still dark when I finally stood up. Across the water it was quiet, the fire had died but the glow from the embers was still visible. I could just see the flickering beam from a torch deep amongst the trees. The need to think clearly whilst battling a beginning hangover. What to do? What *should* I do? My first thought was to get away as soon as possible. But paddling away in my canoe under the moonlight would no doubt reveal my presence if someone was still at the cabin, the splashing sound of the paddle carrying straight across the lake. My next thought was more comforting. Like any prey when threatened, lie completely still. In addition, I was also so tired that it became a foregone conclusion. I put the swag on top of the collapsed tent, crawled into the sleeping bag and fell asleep.

~ ~ ~

Gunnar dragged Steve's body onto a large plastic tarpaulin. Nobody was talking. Vivian could be heard crying inside the cabin. Kai and Peter getting bucket after bucket of water from the lake, pouring it over the flat rocks and scrubbing away at the blood-stains. "Help me carry him", Gunnar said to Joe, who was absentmindedly surveying the scene. Joe reluctantly lifted one edge and together they put the body in the back of the Mercedes.

Earlier there had been much shouting, fights almost breaking out between them, before they all calmed down enough to start discussing what to do; every one of them had a lot at stake. In the end they agreed, they had to conceal the murder. They were all complicit.

Initially it had all gone to plan, Gunnar and Vivian had 'accidentally' run into Steve at a cafe in Oslo. Vivian managing to persuade him to join them for a party at the cabin that same evening. Divorced and childless, Steve had nobody he needed to notify.

It was all pre-arranged to get Steve on board with their plans. Beer, schnapps, crayfish and Vivian, plus the promise of a share option agreement that would give him a slice of the future profits of their venture. It was going well, everyone was in high spirits, but when it came to the crunch, when the question of the approval process came up, the answer was not what they had all been hoping for. Steve did not budge, no amount of persuasion or cajoling would make him change his mind. And that was it. There was no plan B. They all thought he'd cave in the end. And if not, so be it. But not as far as Gunnar was concerned, he had his own plan B. A last resort. Slowly, it emerged that the killing of Steve was not altogether impulsive. Gunnar had destroyed Steve's SIM-card when he went to the toilet at the cafe, meaning that any electronic traces of Steve's whereabouts ended in Oslo around 2pm on the Saturday. This of course indicated a premeditated act, which Gunnar finally admitted. He was responsible, carrying the burden for the common good, and in return he demanded their silence. If any one of them cracked, they would all suffer the consequences, their venture never to be realised. In the end greed won. As it always does.

~ ~ ~

When I woke up, it felt like it had all been a dream, a bizarre concoction of fragments ending in a scream. I got out of the sleeping bag. My head was sore and my mouth felt like sandpaper. I craved coffee, the only antidote. Grabbing the kettle I crouch walked down to the water, the dawn light was enough for me to see across to the cabin. It looked deserted, but I couldn't be sure. Five minutes later I was sitting on a log with a hot, life giving coffee cupped in my shivering hands.

Did it really happen? The quarrelling, the shot, what I heard afterwards? Yep, there could be no doubt, someone had been killed over there. I would do best to get away from the island and go to the police. At the same time I was kind of on the run from the police myself. And from Aron. What a mess. I realised that there was no way I could involve myself in whatever had happened. To be the main witness in a murder case not worth contemplating, at least not now. The next three weeks my only focus needed to be getting the money together for Aron. Nothing else.

The island was no longer a place to be. I felt vulnerable and decided to leave just after sunset. That would give me time to eat, recover my wits and ensure that there was nobody left in the cabin. I poured what was left in the kettle into another pot and threw in a couple of snags to boil. They tasted as delicious as only greasy food can do on a hangover, further enhanced by a bottle of beer, I was starting to feel a lot better.

I decided to take advantage of my improved condition, assess my situation and see how I could best get out of Aron's clammy clutches. Unfortunately, the starting point was not great. My assets consisted of a 42 inch flat screen TV, a top quality stereo system and a five year old Audi Quattro. All easy enough to sell to raise some cash, but still a mere pittance in the scheme of things. I had no family and no friends dumb enough to lend me money. Time was short, three weeks flies by, even in bad company.

The only idea left from my earlier ruminations, and not entirely without merit, was to rob Mrs Danielsen. She used to be our neighbour where I grew up, and according to dad, "filthy rich", with mum invariably admonishing him for "foul speech in front of the children", dad answering back that "being rich is not foul" with mum exasperated telling him "you know what I mean". They really could carry on, but still…

Mrs Danielsen had inherited a fortune from her husband. She probably still lived in the same affluent suburb, unless she was dead or in a nursing home. She had always been sort of old, belonging as she did to my grandparents' generation. I had visited her house several times. The paintings on the wall so numerous they almost completely covered the silk wall paper, including an Edvard Munch and many others of similar vintage and value. She always wore diamond rings and a pearl necklace. Nonetheless she was an old witch who had lived a privileged life, about time she experienced some adversity in her twilight years, I thought rather uncharitably.

Breaking in was going to be the easy part, but getting rid of loot like jewellery and paintings for cold, hard cash quite another matter. It would take time, and I didn't have much of that, there would no doubt be shady dealers who would turn a blind eye and buy, but at what price? Ten, maybe twenty percent of the value at best. That would mean I would have to steal fifteen million worth at least, and a robbery like that would cause considerable interest from the police, maybe even the media. Not at all desirable. I needed cash, not loot. And coffee.

I brought the kettle down to fill it again, glanced towards the cabin to check. And then it kind of hit me like an apparition at first. Except it was quite the obvious answer. I just hadn't seen it until that moment. Maybe it was the circumstances, the lack of sleep, the booze, but whatever it was, the solution to my predicament was only about 500 metres away. Next to the cabin. I had witnessed a murder for chrissake. I knew. I had inside information. How much was that worth to those people? I decided it would be worth three million. Sounded reasonable and it would also give me a bit of profit after having repaid Aron. I felt like screaming with relief, which I did, but silently, for quite a while. Then I celebrated with a beer.

For the rest of the day I made sure I stayed half drunk, anxious not to give in to the sobering thought that my plan had quite a few holes in it. What worried me more than anything was why Aron was already on to me, three weeks before the money was due. As the afternoon wore on I started getting restless. I wanted to get away from the island, but I could see some intermittent activity at the cabin so I stayed put. I had only seen three cars leaving. I packed up and got myself ready. Just as the sun disappeared behind the hills a car drove away and the cabin was dark. I followed the car with my eyes until it disappeared. Then it was my turn, I thought about paddling across to the cabin and snoop around, but decided against it. Too risky, what if they had forgotten something and returned? I put my kit in the canoe and pushed off, paddling as silently as I could back to where I'd come from.

Smuggler

I got back without incident, the car was still parked where I'd left it. I wanted to go back to Oslo, but knowing I had been detected in town a couple of days earlier, my apartment was not safe. This was no game, not like trading shares with virtual money, or a video game like Modern Warfare. If I couldn't pay back the money, I owed I had no doubt the repercussions would be brutal. I could not know what sort of contacts and IT resources Aron had access to, but I had seen enough episodes of CSI, NCIS and other police 'procedurals' to take serious precautions. Consequently, where to take shelter for the night was no trivial matter. It had to be with someone living alone, someone not close to me, someone who could not be traced back to me, yet still someone who knew me well enough to take me in. There were a few candidates I could think of, but one stood out: Andy. Andy and I were drinking buddies, I'd run into him in different bars and nightclubs. We'd talk, laugh and get drunk together, but we had never exchanged mobile numbers or become Facebook friends, simply because Andy didn't have a mobile or a computer. Refused to, didn't want to succumb to modern life, he still paid by cheque, but preferred cash. He was a shoemaker.

During the drive I recapped what had happened to me over the last few weeks. It had started with something as banal as an illegal consignment of imported spirits. Not a big deal in my book, just selling a legal commodity to people who refused to pay the exorbitant prices of the state Wine Monopoly. Opportunistic, yes, maybe even a bit idealistic, and certainly not criminal. But nevertheless I found myself with 2.5 million in smuggling debt, money I just didn't have. If I did have them, I wouldn't have smuggled anything in the first place. When all is said and done money is the lowest common denominator in our society. You can get anything with money, even happiness. Only those without imagination don't agree, I reasoned.

I had done it before. A semi-trailer load of spirits imported from Poland had financed my four years of business school, including partying and holidays. I had lived like a king, enjoyed every minute of it, and got my education debt free, unlike most of my contemporaries. After a failed attempt as an online entrepreneur peddling a weight-loss program, I got a nine-to-five job at a wholesale food import company. With a salary of about half a million a year, the tax man taking his 50%, my apartment costing about 12,000 per month, after car expenses and food I had almost no money left over for a beer on Saturday evening. What kind of life was that?

I lasted about two years. Then I thought how about another trip to Poland? Last time had been such a success. I went through the same process and contacts and organised a delivery promising me around 50% profit. As a salaried employee I trundled along to the bank, hat in hand so to speak, and asked for a loan of two million. But without collateral there wasn't much to gain from that. Tried some other avenues with the same result, until a few other swings and roundabouts led me to Aron, who lent me the two million straight away. At 25% interest over 60 days. "Your kneecaps is my collateral" he said with an ominous smile revealing his gold tooth competing for attention with the other bling he wore around his neck and on his fingers. Fat pig I thought to myself. And Aron had never attended business school, so when he said 25% that was exactly what he meant. 25% of the two million was 500,000, notwithstanding a 60 day loan term making the annual interest rate 381%. I didn't like it, but I knew what I was doing, or rather I was blinded by the pot of gold at the end of the rainbow as so often before.

The semi-trailer would enter Norway from Sweden, on one of the 87 border-crossings, of which only 21 are permanently controlled. An acquaintance suggested a particularly remote crossing that had not been subject to any controls for more than ten years. I went there to scout it myself on three different occasions and it looked equally deserted on both sides of the border every time. I checked again only hours before the trailer was due, same deal. But when it arrived, on schedule, a whole team of customs agents emerged from the derelict old weatherboard toll booth. Everything was confiscated; they had obviously been tipped off. I had heard whispers that some of the regular smugglers would rat on others to help the customs officials reach their quotas and then turn the other way. As a novice, I was an easy target, and there was nothing I could do about it. Well, not a complete novice, having used false identities along the way, police would have a hard time tracking me down. But that was little consolation, my debt to Aron of 2.5 million would not go away, and it was due in a little over three weeks. I had no doubt that my kneecaps would be subjected to severe damage if I didn't pay on time. The big, bald guy chasing me down the street the other day was not fast enough to catch me just because his tree-trunk like thigh muscles slowed him down. The mere thought of him sent shivers down my spine.

En route to Oslo I returned the canoe and grabbed a bite to eat at a roadside tavern. Andy lived in an old workers cottage on the outskirts of town, I had been there more than once for a few nightcaps after an evening on the skids. It was almost ten o'clock at night when I knocked on the door.

"Marius, eh?" He was surprised, but after a slight hesitation he welcomed me in. Typically Andy, unkempt, unshaven, hair too long, eyes drowsy, not exactly a chick magnet. But what he lacked in outward appearance he made up for with originality. "Thanks, Andy, thanks a lot", I took off my shoes and stepped into his living room. It was like stepping back in time, or into a museum. Except for the "modern" amenities of a radio and a turntable, the room was adorned by colourful old rugs, an odd assortment of furniture pieces, a brocade table cloth and ceramic crockery in green and orange. I sunk down into the velour sofa. "Want a beer? Look like you need one!" Without waiting for an answer he went into the kitchen and returned with two bottles. "What a surprise visit, nice to see you, what's up?" He feigned interest, but dull and tired eyes gave him away.

"Thanks", I said as I grabbed the bottle. "Well nothing much really, just need a place to crash for the night. Just tonight, I promise. But no questions, please, I just can't answer them. Not right now anyway. But when the time is right, I'll tell you a story you won't forget! That I can promise!"

"Looking forward to it already", he said as he sat down on an old brown beanbag that had seen better days. "Cheers!"

Island Gypsy

By ten o'clock the next morning, I was seated at a suburban cafe with a coffee and a tasty sandwich. I'd reactivated my mobile for long enough to call work and extend my sick leave. "Yeah, sorry, still have a bad cough and a bit of a temperature", indicated it would be a few more days and reassured them I'd get a doctor's certificate organised.

I deliberately found a table at the back. Across from me I noticed a young pretty blond girl, a student. Business studies I guessed, probably marketing. The cute ones stayed away from the quantitative disciplines, and if they were pretty enough, they'd always be hired by some drooling HR director. That's life, bloody unfair. The trick is to avoid being a victim to it. The blond stood up, swayed her hips as she walked out, off to the first study group for the day, I guessed.

I took another bite of the sandwich, connected my laptop to the WiFi and started browsing the news sites. Nobody had been reported missing, nobody found dead. No surprises there, too early for that. More surprising was that there had still been no mention of a semi-trailer load of illegal spirits having been intercepted at the Swedish border.

Through Google Maps and the official property registry I found the actual address of the cabin, and then it was easy enough to identify the owner - Gunnar Fergusen. Another Google search revealed him as the owner of a company - Water Pressure Systems P/L - specialising in the sealing of concrete. The business registry told me he was one of two board members - the other was Vivian Fergusen. Gunnar and Vivian, both names that had reverberated across the water on Saturday evening. No doubt, he was my man, the killer.

Not for the first time I marvelled at the incredible transparency of Norwegian society - you can't hide anything, it's all on public record, even your tax return! A bit more searching and I found that Gunnar owned a house in the more affluent part of town, not far away from where I grew up, plus another in the eastern suburbs, near the cabin. Promising, and then I hit pay-dirt. Gunnar Fergusen was the Vice President of the Princess Yachts' Owners Club of Oslo. In other words, in addition to owning two houses and a cabin, he is also the proud owner of a Princess, one of the most prestigious and over-priced floating 'gin palaces' money can buy! Sure enough, as I clicked through to the website and found the photographs of smug looking, tanned Princess owners, there he was, the man from the dinghy. Handsome, well-trimmed beard and wavy hair, white teeth and smiling eyes, didn't look at all like a murderer. The photograph caption confirmed it, number four from the left, Gunnar Fergusen. Finally, I went to the tax department site and found him to have net income of 1.7 million last year, and net assets of 12.4 million.

I ordered a beer, not to celebrate, but to quell the uneasy feeling in my stomach. If I was going to succeed in blackmailing Gunnar Fergusen, I needed a bit of elbowroom and time. I just couldn't do it looking over my shoulder every step of the way. The beer did the job of soothing my nerves so I had another. I put the SIM card back in my phone before getting in the car, I wanted to be on the move while talking to Aron, just in case he was able to track my mobile.

He answered after just two rings - "well if it isn't Marius Tokle himself, about time" - his voice menacing. If not for a couple of beers I might have hung up there and then, but I steeled myself: "Why is that? Why are you chasing me? The money is not due for another three weeks!" I felt I had to be on the offensive, respond in the same way, show him I wasn't one to mess around with.

"Don't you think I know what happened? How are you

going to come up with 2.5 million in less than three weeks? Tell me that, you fuckin' smart-arse!" How the hell did he know? He was right, of course, but why did he want to get hold of me now? Threatening me or beating me up wouldn't help his cause, would it? Then he might not get paid at all. Either way, I had to stay defiant. "Listen, Aron, you're right, it turned to shit. But I've still got 450,000, money I was going to give to the driver after he crossed the border, and I still have time to find the balance. I'll do it, I have a plan, but I'll need to be able to work in peace, so hold back your gorillas, put them in a cage and let me get on with it. Deal?"

"What kind of plan?" His voice still sarcastic, but I could tell he was curious.

"I can't tell you, and it's none of your business. What matters is that you'll get your 2.5 million in three weeks, alright?" He didn't say anything for a while, made me wonder if he was just plain stupid, bat shit crazy, or super smart. Was he actually thinking, or was he just sitting there gaping, salivating out of the corner of his mouth?

"OK, I'll give you a deal you can live with, Marius. But the circumstances have changed. Smuggling spirits into Norway is what I consider low risk, hence I gave you the loan. But you still fucked it up. Why would I believe you now, you won't even tell me your plan? So my risk has increased, so has the interest rate. So the deal is now three million in three weeks. You went to business school so you get the picture." I was stunned, he was definitely not stupid, and worse still, I knew he was right. But double the interest was just not fair. Not fair at all.

"What? Are you crazy, Aron? If I give you back your 2.5 million in three weeks, we are square. I have kept my side of the bargain, end of story!"

"But what if you fuck up again?"

"Doesn't help if I owe you another 500,000 then, does it?"

"That's your problem, not mine. And pay attention, young man, I said I'd give you a deal you could live with, didn't I..."

Fuck me dead, what a dirty scumbag, I thought, as I

realised there was no point in trying to negotiate further. I had to accept the "offer" or not. I'd still be left with the 450,000 if I used the full amount of the blackmail money to settle with Aron. Maybe I could up the ante with Fergusen? Either way, I had no option but to accept. "Alright then, Aron, three million in three weeks. But you keep your gorillas away from me. If I see that big bald thug again the deal is off!"

"You just don't get it, do you Marius, I am calling the shots here. And I want to be able to call you 24/7."

No fucking way, I hung up.

I drove towards town, steering with my left hand as I removed the SIM card with the right. It wasn't even midday and I had already lost half a million. Didn't know if I could afford to live much longer. Ten minutes later I was sitting at a dank, old pub with my third pint for the day. I wasn't alone, but managed to blend in with the dirty brown walls and the other early drinkers, listening to Louis Armstrong's hoarse voice telling us what a wonderful world it was. Somewhat contrasting the feeling that Aron had his hands around my balls, ready to squeeze hard if I didn't do as he told me to. The feeling was that he would prefer to rip them off rather than get his money back. That's what scared me the most. Having him breathing down my neck over the next few weeks would just not work. He was clearly mad. What would he do if he got hold of me? Would he break my arm or crush a kneecap? Or worse? My only hope was to get the money.

So I needed a place to sleep, a place to work out how to execute my plan. My apartment was not a good option after having talked to Aron. Then I had a sudden thought, remembering that my good mate Brad had told me a little while ago that his boat would be left unattended during the winter as he was going sailing in the Caribbean; so could I check up on it from time to time? He had left a key in the usual place. The boat was a converted trawler, around 40 feet, and fully equipped as a live-aboard, bunks for eight, full pantry, a fridge and heating. And I still had the sleeping bag in the back of my car.

I nodded to the bartender as I left; always tried to stay friendly with the guardians of God's liquid. Felt a bit tipsy, but in the scheme of things driving under the influence seemed rather trivial. I also thought of myself as one of those people who drive better with a few, although not many practised it anymore after zero tolerance came into effect a few years ago.

But I did; frequently, and yet again without incident. Not long after I was at Kings Marina on the east side of the bay. The weather was changing, a bit of drizzle and a brisk southerly breeze coming off the fjord. I shuddered as I walked out towards the neatly laid out marina berths. Brad's boat was in its usual spot, the 'Island Gypsy'. A boat with real pedigree, but still looked out of place between a three-storey Fairline and a sleek Swan.

I found the key as expected in a little hollow right under the top of the wheelhouse. As I got inside and stepped down into the cabin below, the stale air rose to greet me. It was dark as I fumbled to find the light switch. The single lamp above the chart table gave the cabin a faded look, not unlike the pub I had just left. Maybe that's why Brad liked it so much, I mused, but the important thing was that there was power. There was an old diesel stove and an electric oven on the floor was radiating enough heat to keep the interior from freezing during the coming winter months. Then I felt a slight movement, almost imperceptible, but contrary to the natural movement caused by the moderate swell or the wind. I stood absolutely still, listening intently. I heard someone starting to push the door open, I grabbed a knife from the top drawer in the pantry, and turned the light off. What now?

"Anyone there?" The voice was friendly, relaxed. I hesitated. "I am on the boat in the next berth, thought I heard

footsteps, just checking, we look after each other around here."
Made sense, boaties are like that.

"Hello", I said, and turned the light back on, "I'm down here", I looked up towards the door. An elderly man, maybe around 70, wearing a captain's hat and a fisherman's sweater. "Hi, I'm a friend of Brad. He asked me to check on his boat while he is sailing in the Caribbean. My name is Marius", I said as I stretched my hand out in greeting. We shook hands as he came into the cabin. "I'm Jon Lauritzen, just wanted to check, there's been a few burglaries in the marina recently."
"That's no good, mate, thanks for being vigilant!"
"No worries, I'll let you go, see you later", he said as he turned around back up the stairs.
"By the way", I called after him, "I'm redecorating my apartment at the moment so I'll probably stay here for a few weeks, just so you know."
He ducked his head back down. "That's nice, please come over for a drink one night. I'm in the 'Fairline' next to you." Then he was gone.

I sat down and looked around my temporary home. This was going to work out fine, I thought.

~ ~ ~

Aron kept pushing. Unbridled muscle power on one side, a concrete floor on the other, flesh, bone and organs in the middle. The victim gasping for air. Tears, snot and sweat running down his face, eyes bulging like a freshly caught fish. Aron kept on pushing until he heard cracking, not unlike the sound of him cracking his knuckles, but this time it was ribs breaking, three, four, five, six. That's enough. He eased off and the man collapsed under him. Heaving for air, each breath resulting in excruciating pain, an impossible dilemma. Aron had perfected the method over the years, he wasn't known as 'The Vise' for no reason. The advantage was that it didn't leave any visible marks on the body to speak of, only a few lesions, making it hard to prove assault. Besides, the victim would be able to function again after a few days on strong pain-killers, often quite important. As it was in this case.

Thor and Vladimir drove the man home, whilst Carl and Aron drove back to the office at Torpedo Pizza. Carl brought Aron up-to-date with what they had found out about Marius: "Firstly, he has no family. His parents and a sister were killed in a car accident eight years ago. He was seventeen at the time. He has an uncle and a cousin, but she got married and moved to Australia, including daddy."

"Sorry to hear that", Aron drawled, "for me, I mean, family always work best. What else?"

"He works for a company that sells hydraulic pumps. About 50 employees. He is their logistics manager. Been there two years. Been on sick leave for a week."

"Sick leave", Aron demurred, "on the run, tail between his legs, more like it. What about women?"

"None on the scene at the moment. Get the impression he is a bit of a party-goer, lots of women, but no attachments. Same goes for friends - lots, but not a best buddy. Lives alone. Plays football Tuesday and Thursday night with old mates from business school."

"So, what you are telling me, Carl, you still haven't found anything we can use?"

Carl swallowed a couple of times before answering, "Not yet, but we will, as you always say Aron, everyone has a weakness, just gotta' find it."

"Yeah, that's it, gotta' find it." Aron rubbed his big hands together staring straight ahead. "I want to get hold of this punk NOW. Nobody hangs up on me!"

I saw you

After having moved my car a few blocks away from the marina, parking in a quiet cul-de-sac, I got my sleeping bag and what was left of my supplies. As I walked back to the marina, the wind had picked up considerably, heavy rain slapped my face and I had to twist my body at an angle to the wind to avoid falling over. Autumn in Oslo. But it still felt quite right; if Aron somehow discovered my car he would have no way of immediately linking it to the marina, and if I got caught on the marina I had a pretty straight escape route back to the car. Pleased to have found a safe refuge, I threw my sleeping bag onto the queen size bed in the aft cabin. Accompanied by the wind howling through the shrouds and the sound of the waves I curled up and fell into a long overdue deep sleep.

When I awoke, I felt reborn. My head and my body kind of vibrating together at some primal frequency that I only ever experienced with a hangover. A state of mind I found especially suitable for analysis and decision making. Consequently, one hour later I was in a small nondescript suburban menswear store with two thoughts in my head. One was to avoid popular public places as much as possible. The second to make myself unrecognisable. I tried on hooded sweaters, hats and baggy jeans. For starters I didn't even recognise myself in the mirror, even without the new clothes. The three day stubble had grown into a scraggy beard, my hair lifeless and dull without the usual gel, and my eyes hollow with dark shadows. Did I look older than my 25 years? I was just about at that stage of life where looking older was becoming a negative. But right now it was a good thing. I ended up purchasing two outfits, some boxer-shorts and socks, and two pairs of Converse sneakers. Even though it felt funny with the seat of my pants hanging below the knees, I thought I appeared quite inconspicuous as I left the store looking like a Snoop Dogg clone.

Ten minutes later I was sitting at Peppes Pizzeria, an old favourite, plus they had free WiFi. Time to start ensnaring Gunnar Fergusen. But first I quickly browsed the news sites, still nothing on missing persons or dead bodies. Then I googled Fergusen again, found his email on the Princess Yachts Owners Club website, I'd need that. I returned to the photographs on the site, lots of photos with Gunnar in party mode, including one from the aft deck of his yacht, "Sunset III". The caption said "Vivian, Gunnar and Beatrice Fergusen among the revellers at the annual club cruise to Fjalbacka", an idyllic village on the Swedish coast. I zoomed in on Beatrice. She was gorgeous; long, platinum blond hair, perfect white teeth, the bluest of blue eyes and a bikini top that revealed a lot more than it covered. And I knew her! Crazy! She was one of those girls at my business school that a mere mortal bloke like me wouldn't dare to even talk to. I wasn't exactly backward in coming forward, but some women could take my self-confidence away just by looking at me. She was one of those. Not that it mattered much now, it was her dad I was after, not her.

My pizza arrived with a glass of Coke. Not taking any risks by not being fully alert at this point. I had to decide how much to demand from Fergusen for keeping my mouth shut about what I had witnessed. My initial thought had been three million, but now that Aron had upped the ante from the two and a half I thought I owed, to three million, it left me with just the 450,000 I still had. The question was how much Fergusen was worth, or more importantly, how much cash could he raise in three weeks? Cash was not as straightforward as it used to be. But it wasn't just him, of course, he had accomplices that were there witnessing the murder. It had been Gunnar and his wife, Vivian. I had heard the names Joe and Kai mentioned a few times, and the victim, Steve. Just the five of them. I had an inkling there had been a couple more. So seven in total, the murderer, the victim, and five witnesses. Could I demand five million then? How much was Gunnar's Princess yacht worth?

I returned to the photographs on the website. There she was again, Beatrice. Oh my God, she was gorgeous! Almost painful to look at, but at the same time there was something about her smile, looked contrived, even strained. Whatever. "Sunset III" wasn't one of the biggest of the Princess Yachts, I was guessing between 40 and 45 feet. On the Yachtsales website I found a Princess 42 for sale, four years old, offered for 2.8 million. I had expected more, but boat sales had slowed down considerably after the global financial crisis of 2008, even in affluent Norway, and there were many boats for sale. And the wrong time of year to sell a boat, having to rush through a sale during autumn and he might only get two million for it. Also, I didn't want to get too greedy. After all my objective was to get out of the pickle I was in with life and limbs intact. Everything else was less important, even the prospect of making a lot of money. If I asked for more than Fergusen and his accomplices could muster, or they refused to pay, then I was the one in trouble. So I decided on discretion being the better part of valour and settled for three million.

I had to go for a piss; brought my laptop with me and headed for the men's room. Someone called out "Marius?" Without thinking I turned around, immediately realising my mistake as I should have continued walking. I looked straight at Britt Wangen, secretary and chief gossiper at my work. Shit a brick.

"Marius, what on earth are you wearing?" She started laughing, "what happened, mid-life crisis come early?"

"Nah…" I started, but was lost for words, so after a few awkward seconds I managed only a feeble "how did you recognise me?"

"Not quite sure" she said with a wry smile, "maybe your

gait, you kinda' sway when you walk. And your nose poking out through the hood. You have a rather characteristic nose."

How ridiculous. I had done everything to be anonymous and then I was recognised within an hour! Although Britt did know me, knew my profile, how I walked. Aron's foot soldiers didn't have that advantage, at least.

"But are you not supposed to be sick? You will need a doctor's certificate, you know." She was looking at me, spitefully, knowing full well she had caught me out.

"Yeah, I am sick, just needed to get out for a bit, get some food into me. Of course I'll get a doctor's certificate!", turned around and continued to the toilet. Oh well, that's the end of that job, most likely. Britt would tell everyone at work, no doubt, and that would be all my boss needed to get rid of me. Fair enough. Didn't like it much there, anyway.

I returned to my table. Britt had gone. Time to put things in motion. To start with, I needed to set up an incognito email account. After a bit of thought I registered "isawyoumate@gmail.com". That should pique the interest of the recipient. I started typing:

"Gunnar, I was there on Saturday. Close enough to hear you guys talking about wolves, crayfish and drunken trips to Sweden. You, Vivian, Joe and Kai. And Steve. I know you fired the shot. One word to the police and all hell will break loose.

"My silence will cost you three million in cash, large bills only. I could ask for more, but don't want to be unreasonable. Unless you try to bargain with me, then I will be. You've got two weeks. Maybe you'll have to sell 'Sunset III'. Start working. Tick tock, tick tock."

My hands got sweaty. Not so strange, I sensed I was poking a sleeping bear. But I didn't have a choice. I added "STEVE IS DEAD" in the subject field to make sure there'd be no doubt. I was addressing him on a first name basis as if we knew each other. Ah well, I moved the cursor over the send button, hovered there for a bit, my finger suspended for a few seconds, then I clicked. The audible "swish" of the Gmail app sounded ominous, the point of no return.

Gunnar

As per usual, Gunnar Fergusen stopped at the "Red Goat" on his way to work, a coffee stall modelled on the wheelhouse of an old fishing trawler, right in the middle of the urban marketplace not far away from where he lived. It was known to have the best coffee in town. Even on a cold autumn day with strong and icy wind gusts, people would queue up for 15 minutes or more just to get their favourite cuppa'. In addition, Gunnar thought it was important to stick to his daily routine after what had happened last weekend. Business as usual. At home was another story, although the periods between the hysterical outbursts by Vivian were getting longer.

When he arrived at the office, he took the time for a chat with a couple of the sales guys before settling down at his desk with a fresh coffee and turned on his PC. Twenty unread emails, mostly spam and marketing. No, he didn't need the latest in power tools, nor go on some motivational junket or an exotic holiday; Isawyoumate@gmail.com, more spam. He was just about to hit delete when he gave out an audible gasp as he read the subject line - "STEVE IS DEAD". He trembled as he opened it.

~ ~ ~

I woke up around midday, head sore and tongue dry as sandpaper. Arriving home the day before, I ran into Jon from the boat next to me, and he asked me in for a drink. I then heard the story of the life of a man who had been burning the candle at both ends for a very long time, with nothing but a short candlestick left. Three marriages, eight kids with five different women and no contact with any of them. Drinking himself to oblivion and the loss of properties and what was once a substantial business with more than 100 employees. The boat was the only thing he had left. I liked him, I liked him a lot. And that was part of his problem, he was a charismatic character, charming, but not good at anything. The result inevitable. Now just a poor old drunk, I felt for him. Last thing I did before leaving him was to cover him with a blanket as he fell asleep on the couch in the elegant, but somewhat tired and worn cabin of the Fairline.

As I stepped out to refill my water tank I peered in to see if Jon was there; at least he wasn't on the couch where I'd left him. I hoped he had made it to his bed. Back on my boat I turned on the gas and soon I had a hot coffee in my hand. Found a bottle of brandy and poured some into my mug to take the edge off the hangover. There is something special about having a coffee on board a boat. Maybe it's just because when you are on a boat, it's free time, and you feel free. Or maybe it's the whiff of wood and diesel that brings out the best in the coffee. Coffee feels good in a fibreglass boat, too, but still not quite the same.

I tried refocusing on yesterday's events. Did I jump the gun? Should I have asked for more? Ten million? Why not? How often do you get a chance like this in life? Never again, most likely. And there I was, hat in hand, demanding a measly three million. I got angry, banged my fist on the table, where did this bashfulness come from?

It made me think of the traditions of the old Persian empire. Before every important decision, such as whether to go to war or not, the generals advising the Shah would drink themselves into a stupor and then discuss the options. They would then sleep off the alcohol to reconvene and discuss it again. They would do this until they came to the same conclusion both sober and drunk. I reckon the Persians were onto something important, the value of seeing a situation from every angle. And it was a fair indication that I just didn't drink enough, and this could end up costing me millions. Fuck that!

It took a few minutes before Gunnar fully grasped the content of the email he had just received. At first he thought it was just a bad joke. A very bad joke. But his shirt was stuck to his back with sweat. Which one of the boys would have the temerity to do that? He had known them all since primary school, none of them would be even close to being that bold or callous. And if it wasn't any of the boys, then this was serious. It meant someone had been out there in the vicinity Saturday night. Or more than one. Witnesses. He felt like his guts were about to be turned inside out. With a groan he started running towards the toilet, hand on his mouth, but he only got as far as the reception area before a mixture of coffee and bile came out like a geyser.

Ten minutes later, after quite a bit of kerfuffle, words of sympathy and gentle slaps on the back, Gunnar was back in his office by himself. The stomach cramps persisted and he hunched over the desk in pain. He opened the email again, the fuckin' blackmailer must have been close to the cabin. He knew a lot of details. He was only missing Peter, otherwise he was spot on. Gunnar considered going back out to the cottage to have a look around. He'd do that later. And the amount: three million, in cash. Could he even do that? "Maybe you'll have to sell Sunset III?" Could it be someone he knew? Someone from the boating fraternity? But with everything available online it meant nothing. But there was something about how the email was written. People from the district around the lake would not use a phrase like "don't want to be unreasonable". That was someone from Oslo, more specifically from the better part of town, from his own neighbourhood. But the thought of any of his neighbours having followed him out to the cottage to hide in the woods was as good as unbelievable. Moreover, the email was written by someone educated, it was just like his own financial controller would have written it. In other words, an academic from the west end of Oslo - the 'right' side of the tracks.

First thing he had to do was to call a meeting. He needed them all there. One for all, all for one. He sent them all an email requesting them to meet him at his office that night, at 8pm. Then he left the office, told his receptionist he wasn't feeling well and needed to go home. But instead he drove east, through the city tunnel, and then further east towards the lake. Gunnar always felt he could think better on the move, not behind a desk. And he desperately needed to think. It just seemed so unlikely that anyone had been there spying on them on purpose. It could have been a moose hunter who had gotten lost in the woods and seen the fire. But if so, he would have walked right up, happy to have found people to help him. And it was too late in the season for campers and fishermen. Besides, he had checked; there were nobody to be seen in any of the other cottages, nobody on the little island, either. So what about... Nah, too far fetched, but he still mulled over it for a bit. Had he been too naive? He did know Kai, Joe and Peter since primary school. But everything had changed after what happened. How did they see him now? A murderer, or the one doing whatever it would take to make them all rich? Was one of them trying to take advantage of the situation? Blackmail him. And why the amount of three million? He'd already calculated it was just what he'd be able to scrape together in cash within a couple of weeks. Peter had flippantly intimated a few times that it would be Gunnar who would benefit first, take less of a risk, make the most and contribute the least. How serious was he about that? Serious enough to do this? He didn't want to believe it, but couldn't rule it out, either. What was the most likely scenario here, that their protagonist was a coincidental bystander, or one of those present at the scene? Reluctantly, he found the latter to be more likely.

He was getting close to the cottage now, exited the main highway and started the ascent. The half hour drive through forest and undulating grazing land was usually becalming for him, but not today. The closer he got, the tighter the grip around the wheel, so when he arrived at the cottage his neck was tight and his shoulders sore. He got out of the car rather gingerly and walked out to the headland where the bonfire had been. The cold wind was whipping up angry little waves flying across the lake and slapping against the rocks. The tall fir trees behind the cottage swayed like drunken giants. So this is where he had shot Steve only three days earlier.

It seemed like such a long time ago, he suddenly doubted if it had ever happened at all. Steve. A friend from kindergarten, then through school and the ever reliable goalkeeper for their local football team. A rival for the attention of Vivian throughout high school, and now - after so many years - the unmovable obstacle between himself and more money that he could expect to make in a lifetime. Did he regret it? Nope. A sole individual against progressing their local community, employment opportunities, economic growth, no, he couldn't accept that. Steve had been given a very reasonable offer. No, he didn't regret it. Not that. But he did regret not checking the area more thoroughly beforehand.

He looked around. The cottage was surrounded by a dense forest. Someone could easily have hidden beneath some branches and seen it all, from less than 50 metre away. But why? He had not told anybody about his plans in case Steve resisted, not even Vivian. He could not understand, but someone had been there, so he had to start looking.

He changed his clothes and shoes, started zigzagging between the trees but found nothing but moose droppings and a rusty cigarette lighter. He walked back out on the headlands. He had surveyed the lake on the night as he started realising where things were heading. No lights from any of the other cottages, no activity to be seen or heard from the island. In the old days he remembered how he and Vivian had enjoyed sitting outside during balmy summer evenings, listening to the kids partying out there, and at other times they could make out the sounds of the wood grouse performing its mating dance in the distance. So he knew how far sounds travelled and that they easily could have been heard on the island. But he had checked the island, too, at least what he could see from the dinghy.

He would have to row out there, as the outboard had been taken home for winter storage when they left. His sore shoulders made rowing a struggle, not helped by the wind pushing him off course and the waves splashing over the side, wetting his pants. By the time he got to the island he was wet and cold, fingertips stiffened and blue. He cursed everything and everybody as he jumped up and down to regain some warmth. There were footmarks in the sand. Nothing he could identify, but clear enough indication that someone had been here within the last few days. Unusual, this time of year. He recognised the beer-can tree, a few more condoms on it since he had last been out here. He continued up the east side of the island, towards the best camp-site, that gets the early morning sun. There was a fire-pit with a rockbed and a neatly constructed square of notched logs. A stack of firewood nearby. Not a single piece of paper, not an empty bottle in sight, not even a cork or a cap, as if someone pedantic had taken possession of the place and maintained it. Maybe to use it all year around. He would need to check with the local farmer, Kaare, he kept tabs on pretty much everything that happened. On the north side of the island there was nothing so he walked straight across to the west side, the side facing his cottage. Kept walking down to the water's edge, a perfect spot to observe what had been happening. On a windless evening like it had been on Saturday night, the sounds would have travelled unfettered across the water.

He started searching the area more closely. On a small branch he found what looked like a chicken bone, still with a bit of meat on it. He sniffed at it, didn't smell much, most likely it would only be a few days old. He could also see that the grass had been flattened in places. Beneath the old fir-tree on the shore he could make out some illegible scribblings in the coarse sand. Someone had definitely been there. Right where he was standing. A mixture of excitement and anger was welling up inside him. He kept searching but didn't find anything else of note. Then, as he was making his way back towards the dinghy he saw something shiny, halfway hidden behind a rock. A bottle of Jack Daniel's. There was still a bit left in the bottle, he unscrewed the cap and sniffed. A sweet, smoky smell filled his nostrils.

He had a strong feeling of having found the 'hotbed'. To get even closer to the person he was looking for, he quickly downed what was left in the bottle. "Yuck" he almost gagged, "bloody girlie drink", almost as sweet as a liqueur. What did it say about who had been here? Was he feminine, or maybe he was a she? Why not? Either way, he had an inkling he would soon find out.

~ ~ ~

I felt quite safe on the boat. But I was restless, so when the evening came I had to get out. In my disguise I felt quite inconspicuous, even if Britt had recognised me. I would wait a few days before contacting Fergusen again, let him stew on his predicament for a while, allow the realities to sink in. Above all I was wondering if and when Steve would be reported missing and the media get involved. It had been three days since he was murdered. Someone would be missing him by now? But as I got onto the internet at a cafe, I couldn't find anything, only the usual stories of politicians quarrelling over stuff they mostly agree on.

More or less unconsciously, but not quite, as I drove back I positioned myself so that if I turned right, I'd be heading back to the marina, but if I turned left, I'd be going towards my apartment. It would have been useful to retrieve some things from home, but not imperative. The right hand lane was a bit congested, but the left was empty and the green arrow made my decision easy. Some decisions make themselves, legacy of my fascination with the 'Dice Man' by Luke Rhinehart.

I parked the car a few blocks away, and with my cap drawn down almost over my eyes and the hood tied tightly, I sauntered down the side-street. As I got there, a woman came out the entrance, so I managed to get in before the door shut. The staircase had windows facing the street, I walked up to the landing between the third and fourth floor. From there I could see the door to my apartment on the third. I normally kept a light on in the hallway which would also be seen in the living room, but it was dark. There had been four days since I was there so the lightbulb could have gone out. But if Aron's man was in there, why would he turn off the hallway light? Maybe because of shadows? Or was it more likely he or they were sitting in a car on the street outside? I couldn't see that from here. But then I did see something. A slight glimmer of light from the apartment. No more than a second, maybe from a mobile phone, or a lighter? Someone lighting a joint? If he'd been there since Friday, the wait would have been long enough without slowing it down further, I thought. But either way, there was someone there. Again I had this creepy feeling that Aron would rather beat me up than get his money back. It scared me more than anything - beyond my comprehension.

~ ~ ~

On his return from the cottage Gunnar stopped by the house of the local farmer to find out if he had seen any strangers around lately. He explained that someone had tried to break into his cottage and asked if Kaare had seen anything. He said he had not. But he had seen a black station wagon parked with a roof-rack, a Toyota, or maybe an Audi, they all look alike these days. It had been parked off the old track by the southern inlet. When asked who owned the stacked firewood, he said that he and his ice fishing mates used the spot as their base when catching pike during winter. Kaare proudly pointed to the wall mounted skeleton of what had been an 18 kilogram pike they had caught last winter, the biggest catch since the war. Gunnar said thanks and goodbye, and got back in his car, a little bit wiser.

The mere thought that it could have been one of the boys gave him a bad taste in his mouth. They had been friends all their lives. Through school, football, drinks and girls, then cars and then a concoction of all of it. That's how he remembered it. Joe was the kind and gracious one, best man to everyone, always available, always helpful, always accommodating and agreeing with whoever spoke last. No way it was him. Kai was the world champion, at least in his own mind. Full of ideas, grand plans, but impatient and never able to create anything that lasted. Maybe he couldn't wait any longer, seizing the opportunity? He could be that stupid. That left Peter. Doubtful. Peter is smart. He gets the big picture, sees the opportunities ahead.

Or maybe they were all in on it? A conspiracy? A million each. Maybe they now regarded him as nothing more than a murderer, one they could control and manipulate to do their bidding. No, they wouldn't dare. They wouldn't fucking dare...

It was 7:30pm. The office was empty. Gunnar had made four copies of the email and placed them around the boardroom table. He would meet them at reception, see if any one of them was particularly nervous with sweaty palms or flickering eyes. He went to the bathroom, splashed cold water on his face. He needed to stay calm. Endeavour to look like he was in full control, the exact opposite of how he felt. Hopefully he'd know by the end of the evening.

They arrived at the same time, eyes flickering and with sweaty palms. Not so strange considering what had happened. But Gunnar kept them wondering for a bit longer, making a can of coffee, small talk, seeing if anyone would give anything away. After 15 minutes he let them into the boardroom, they all sat down and started reading. Gunnar was watching them closely. Kai was the first to break the uneasy silence. "What on earth is this?" Gunnar didn't say anything. He wanted to see how it would play out.

"Is this serious?" Joe said, his voice quivering.

After another uncomfortable pause it was Peter's turn: "For fucks sake, say something, Gunnar. Is this a bloody bad joke, or is it real? You'd better tell us now that you've got us all here."

Gunnar looked at each of them in turn, Joe and Kai looked away, Peter held his gaze. They kept staring at each other for several seconds, like two combatants waiting for the first strike. Then Peter reacted, stood up, lent across the table, grabbed Gunnar by the collar of his jacket, pulled him out of his chair and halfway across the table, his other hand in a fist, raised and ready to strike. "What the fuck is this, Gunnar? You are actually sitting here wondering if one of us is behind this! Have you lost the plot, you fuckin' prick!" He let go of his grip and Gunnar fell to the floor. Kai and Joe was staring at them both like scared kittens.

Gunnar got up, straightened his shirt and jacket, ignoring the ripped collar. "Fuck you, Peter! Have you totally lost it? What are you accusing me of? As if I would suggest one of you is behind this? That's just nuts!"

But Peter was not convinced: "Why the charade out by the coffee machine? Small talk about road construction and the weather when it's obvious that this email was what we came here to talk about?"

"So it's true? You are being blackmailed? Who by?" Kai was already sounding like a beaten man.

Gunnar didn't know what to believe any more. Such a violent reaction from Peter could either mean he felt he had been found out, that he was behind it, or that he was genuinely incensed that Gunnar would even consider accusing any of them of such a betrayal. But he had to let that go for now. He needed to regain control of the situation, if at all possible. He stretched his hands out and looked straight at the others: "Hey, hey, boys, calm down. Nobody is accusing anybody of anything here… OK… And yes, the email is genuine. We have a big problem."

"No", Peter retorted quickly, "you have a big problem. You killed Steve. And whoever he is, he is blackmailing you!"

"It's not so simple any more", Gunnar said matter-of-factly, "you are all accomplices. If this comes out we all go to hell. I'll be convicted of murder, the rest of you for being an accessory to murder, or at best for perverting the course of justice by concealing a murder. I don't know what the penalty is for that, but I'd be surprised if it didn't include a stint in jail. We are all in the same boat, I'm afraid."

Joe, slouched back in his chair by now, close to tears: "We haven't done any killing, Gunnar, it was you…"

"I know that, Joe, but the law will beg to differ. You all made the decision to keep quiet and hide what happened. So if I go, you all go. Might as well accept it." There was a long silence, they were all looking at each other, confused, as if the sun had started setting in the east.

"What I can tell you", Gunnar said, "is that I drove up to the cottage earlier today. There were clear signs that someone had been out on the island in the lake on Saturday night. I found a chicken bone and an empty bottle of Jack Daniel's. You'll recall there was no wind on Saturday, and under those conditions the sounds carry quite easily across the water. The local farmer said he had seen a black Toyota or Audi station wagon with a roof-rack. That's all we've got."

"What about the email address, can we trace that?" At least, Kai, was starting to think a little.

"No", Joe said. He was the IT literate among them. "You can name your account whatever you want. it's totally anonymous. Gmail cannot be traced and cannot be hacked."

"Are you intending to pay?" Peter asked.

"What else can we do? As I said, if he goes to the police, we are all done for. And to be clear, I cannot manage that amount by myself, you'll all have to pitch in. But hopefully we'll find out who he is, and then we can get our money back."

They all started talking at once: "Are we going to pay, too? How much? What do we do if we find him? Are you going to kill him, too? If we give in to him now, he'll just come back for more!"

Again, Gunnar had to try to calm them down. "Listen. Let me finish. Yes, I believe we have to pay. I'll manage two million, you have to come up with the rest. Then we'll see how he proposes to do the handover, but that should give us a chance to find out who he is. The thing is that once he receives the money, he too is guilty of serious crime. Not only of blackmail, but of being witness to a murder without reporting it. If he lives a normal life, has a job, a family, friends, the media pressure will be relentless, in addition to serving time in prison. He'll lose his job, friends, maybe even a spouse. For most people that's catastrophic. So if we find out who it is, I think the problem will solve itself. Start getting the cash together, we need to be prepared. And remember, in five years this will all be forgotten, and we will all be sitting on a small fortune." Gunnar looked around the table, like a salesman having just finished his pitch, but what he saw was not encouraging.

Peter spoke first: "Do you believe your own bullshit, Gunnar? Do you really think this guy would give us our money back if we find him? Would you have done that if you were him?" It was a rhetorical question and he interrupted as soon as

Gunnar started to respond: "Never, Gunnar. Not in a million years. You would be ruthless. Either he takes the money and goes away, or he comes back for more. He's got you by the balls. You have to pay, or else... He is clearly not your typical law abiding citizen, if he was he wouldn't have tried to take advantage of what he saw. He would have gone straight to the police."

"Do you really mean that each one of us should pay more than 300,000? Because you killed Steve?" Kai looked as if he was on his way to his own funeral.

"Listen", Gunnar said again, exasperated, "you may be right, Peter. He may well have us by the balls. All we can do is to see what he comes up with next. But for God's sake I did this not just for me, but for all of us. So we could all get rich one day. And now I'm left in the shit. Yes, Kai, you have to contribute. That goes for you, too, Joe. And Peter. Do you think money like this comes easy? That's not how the world works. You have to take some risks, some sacrifices along the way, otherwise you'll be stuck in the same shithole you were born in. Is that what you want?"

"But to kill Steve..." Joe was still teary, finding it hard to get the words out. "I can't handle it. I haven't slept since it happened. I'm a nervous wreck. At work I just sit there, moping, staring out the window. Nothing is worth this, Gunnar. Nothing."

"Yeah, I get that Joe. That goes for all of us, not to mention for Vivian. So let's just get this over and done with. Anyone wanting to go to the police and give me up?"

Nobody said anything for quite a while, even Peter was staring at the table. They all knew what was at stake. "If not, I suggest that we all go home, empty our mattresses and cookie jars for large bills. Everyone here does a bit on the side, so it shouldn't be impossible. Whatever Peter says, I believe that there is a chance we can get our money back, one way or another. I have to get home to Vivian. It's been a long day."

Steve

Finally! "Local politician reported missing." I started reading: "Steve Hall, a local politician from the Eastern District, was reported missing Tuesday after he didn't attend a council meeting Monday morning. During the day, friends and the police tried contacting Hall without success. Hall is well known as an activist against the protection of wolves and has received death threats for his views. The police is appealing to the public for any information."

The picture was now complete. Steve Hall. Without his consent or knowledge Steve Hall was about to become a donor, a donor of money. Maybe as critical for me as a kidney transplant could have been. Rest in peace, Steve. I couldn't promise him justice, but I could promise him sweet revenge over Gunnar Fergusen. I decided there and then that the price had gone up by a million. That was the least I could do!

To avoid ending up making the same mistake again when making a decision I ordered a beer. Maybe it would be five or six million by day's end? The bartender looked at me quizzically, as if wondering why a grown-up hip-hop dude was having a beer before midday. Maybe I was some kind of obscure celebrity? If only he knew! I took a sip of the beer. How could water, barley, hops and yeast taste so good? And do you so good, too! I googled Steve Hall. 18,500 hits. Not an uncommon name, but easy enough to find relevant information about the one I was after. "High profile Farmers Party politician, Steve Hall, has again received death threats due to his stance on eradicating wolves from Norway once and for all. Hall says 'the indigenous wolf died out more than a 100 years ago, so why should we now introduce a Russian species of wolf into Norway? Wolves are plentiful in vast areas of Russia, from the Atlantic to the Pacific oceans. it's no longer native to

Norway and should be shot.' Such pronouncements have incensed animal protectionists, and last week Hall received an anonymous letter stating: 'You want a bounty on wolves? There is now a bounty on your head. You have been warned.' When asked about the threats, Hall said 'I know there are people out there who value the life of animals higher than that of humans. Yet they eat fish, poultry and meat every day. I can't worry about people like that.'"

Steve Hall was undoubtedly a man of integrity. I recalled that wolves were a topic of discussion on Saturday night, but I doubted very much if that was what lead to him being killed. I continued reading: "Wolves have again been spotted not far from a built-up area, on a road many kids use to get to school. The mother of seven year old Katrina reacted: 'Of course we worry about wolves in our neighbourhood. We are afraid to let the kids out to play in the evening, and we have established a parent group that take turns to follow the kids to and from school.' Steve Hall, the Farmers Party politician, has promised the locals that he will pursue the matter: 'The so called "predators settlement" is a failure, pushed through by ignorant urban politicians in Oslo and Brussels. I'd like to see the headlines when wolves are seen around the outskirts of Oslo West! This is why the Farmers Party wants the wolves removed from areas close to the population centres, and this is why we need a bounty on wolves. it's unacceptable that parents fear for their children's safety like this!'"

He had a point. If you're afraid of wolves, it didn't matter what other people thought! Steve Hall seemed to me like a decent guy with strong opinions. Controversial, but Norway is not the kind of country where people get killed because of a disagreement on animal rights. I kept on searching, following a couple more pieces on wolves, and one where Hall espoused the virtue of growing greens rather than grains.

Then another headline got my attention: "Factory Outlet

Centre proposed for the Eastern District." I honed in: "Local business owners are sick and tired of standing by the highway waving at their customers crossing the border to Sweden to buy cheap goods. This is why they are banding together to create a whole new retail concept, retail stores where the manufacturers can sell direct to the public, bypassing the wholesalers and distributors."

Bjorn Slatto, the leader of the project was quoted saying: "We have to compete, or our whole region is at risk. We need to be able to compete on selection, price and quality, give people a reason not to drive all the way to Sweden. Many of the major brands not currently present in the Norwegian market have expressed a strong interest. Everything from clothing, shoes, furniture, garden tools, around forty different categories. To attract shoppers to come we'll be offering groceries at cost-price, with operating expenses shared between the other tenants. The only thing we won't be able to offer is cut-price alcohol. And what you spend on cheaper petrol in Sweden is lost by driving there, anyway."

The article continued: "The new Factory Outlet Centre will be located around 100 kilometres east of Oslo, just off the main highway, halfway to Sweden. 'Everyone is welcome', Slatto stated with a broad smile. According to Slatto, numerous local businesses are behind the development, but there are also opponents, including Steve Hall, the Farmers Party representative in the local council. 'This is a ridiculous idea, and in the long run it will result in the exact opposite of what its proponents are trying to achieve. If this project is realised, it means the end of local businesses in Askim - the regional capital - and eventually lead to people leaving the district altogether. Moreover, the proposal calls for developing land currently used for farming and forestry, which is totally unacceptable to us. We will fight this.' The Council is scheduled to decide on the issue in early spring next year."

I took another sip of my beer. This was starting to look like something. There was money involved, big money. Enough to kill for? Quite likely. I googled "Factory Outlet Centre" and got 38 hits, the first was the article I had just read, the next two more of the same, but the fourth search result was "Proposal for the Regulation and Impact Statement related to Fergusen North", on the Eastern District Council website. Item 4, ownership, it stated that Gunnar Fergusen was the owner of 81.3% of the total land area of 247 acres.

"Gotcha!", I yelled out, before I knew it. Some people turned around, an older man looked annoyed, a couple of young girls snickering. I gave them the royal wave, and they snickered even more. This was a bit like winning at Lotto. Gunnar Fergusen had killed Steve Hall to get his proposal through the local council. As was often the case, the Farmers Party held the balance of power. And then the relief. I now knew I would be able to pay Aron back. I remained calm, closed my eyes, had a sip of beer. A single tear-drop rolled down my cheek into the corner of my mouth. It had been a long time.

After going to the toilet I ordered another beer. The first beer is great, the second even better, and the third is the best. That's when you enter what athletes call 'the zone', where everything seems to be going on auto-pilot, no thinking, just doing. But the problem with the third is that it often leads to the fourth soon after, and then there is no way back. At least I had the intention that this would be the last one for the day. What interested me now, was the connection between Steve Hall and Gunnar Fergusen, so I googled the names together.

A few hits, a couple where the names appeared in a different context, then one article on the "25-year anniversary of Askim High School". "Last Saturday saw the reunion of the Class of 82 at Askim High. The party started at four with a game of dodge-ball, closely monitored by the now retired gym teacher, Edgar Hansen, before the assembled guest moved to the Old Askim Cafe. 'We have managed to bring 21 out of a class of 25 together. One is sadly deceased, one we were unable to contact, one lives in Australia and one was travelling. In addition, we were fortunate enough to have three of the teachers attending', said one of the organisers, Vivian Fergusen. Then they had their photo taken, of course, where everyone stood in the same position as they did 25 years ago. 'Great fun', said party-goer Kristian Knutsen, 'I am already looking forward to the 50th anniversary!'" Both the old and the new class photos were included.

What struck me looking at the photo from the class of 82, albeit common to all such photos, everyone looks like a dag! They all also included at least one especially attractive girl, who made all the others look plain, and in this photo it was Vivian Nielsen, now Vivian Fergusen, the mother of Beatrice. The same platinum blond hair, the perfect white teeth, the sparkling blue eyes. Right next to Vivian, so close they looked like two heads on the same body, was Gunnar Fergusen, as if he had already 'taken possession' of her. Steve Hall was just in front of them. Crazy to think of, the killer and his victim a metre apart. In the first row on the far left was a dull looking boy, Joe Waller. I had no way of knowing if he was the same Joe as the one present on the fateful night by the lake.

I diverted my attention to the more recent photo from 2007. They all still looked rather daggy, but the jeans and cardigans were replaced by pretty dresses and dark suits, the hairdos either non existent or over-done, and many looked overweight. The most noticeable difference, however, was Vivian, she no longer stood out, she blended, almost faded, in with the rest. Quite sad, really. I wondered why. Gunnar was standing next to her still, but this time there was a clear distance between them. He was one of the few that didn't smile. Maybe a coincidence. Steve Hall had lost all his hair, but he looked strong and full of vitality. Joe was in the same position as in the original photo, still featureless.

I sat there pondering for a little while, finished what was left of the beer. My thoughts were all over the place, nothing concrete. Satisfied with myself and the situation. And then it hit me like I was struck by lightning, the obvious weakness of it all. If I could sit here, at a cafe browsing the internet, and make these connections between Steve Hall, Gunnar Fergusen and the Factory Outlet Centre, so could the police. And if they worked it out, then my inside information would be worthless.

"Fu..." The elderly customer turned around again, obviously still annoyed, but the girls were gone. The saving grace for me was that I *knew* that Gunnar was the killer. I knew what the final picture looked like, but the police had to put the pieces of the puzzle together without such clues. Steve Hall had been subject to death threats. That's where the police would start their investigation. And then they would check any electronic traces of his whereabouts, like his mobile phone records. They would find out that Steve Hall had been at Fergusen's cottage on Saturday night.

From there the connection to the Factory Outlet was easy to make. I had a strong feeling of running out of time. What had they done with the body? And what had they done with his mobile? I just had to get the money from Fergusen before the police solved the puzzle, something I was certain they would do sooner, rather than later. The only thing in my favour was that Fergusen would be painfully aware that it would all unravel from just a few words from me to the police. He would be desperate.

I ordered a third beer. Should I bring the money handover deadline forward? But the less time I gave Fergusen to raise the money, the harder it would be for him to get the cash together, maybe not even enough for me to pay Aron. In the end I concluded that time was of the essence. I had to bring the handover forward and decided against raising the stakes, leaving the demand at three million. Clarity through alcohol. But before I sent my next email, I would have to reevaluate in a state of sobriety.

At this stage I also realised I had gone almost a week without normal, human contact, except for the evening with Andy and the drunken night with Jon. I had only turned on my mobile twice, and that's the way it needed to be until Aron was out of my life. I wasn't game to visit friends or attend football training, in case they too were under surveillance, like my apartment was. So I knocked on the hull of the Fairline and asked Jon to join me for dinner at the Marina Clubhouse. I had eaten there before, standard clubhouse fare, but reasonably priced and decent enough tucker. I had a veal parmigiana and a mineral water, Jon ordered the beef stew and a beer. Our conversation continued where we had left it: heroics and failures, love and betrayals, loss and damnation. If half of Jon's stories were true, he had experienced more in the last few years than most people do in a lifetime.

Like the story of how he proposed to his second wife. He had organised for a table for two to be set up in an idyllic forest setting, white damask, silver cutlery and fine crockery. As they sat down, a waiter appeared out of nowhere with a bottle of champagne and lobster bisque. Ten minutes later a violinist appeared, and not just anyone, a well known musician, playing romantic love songs as Jon went down on his knees, popped the question and got his "yes". And if that wasn't enough, a helicopter appeared above, dropping a thousand red roses and blew the whole setting to kingdom come!

You couldn't make that stuff up. It had to be true. I had to admire this playful and generous man who had approached life head on, taken more than one beating along the way, still adamant he had no regrets. Not that there weren't skeletons in his cupboard, and carnage in his wake, but as he said as we walked back to our boats: "Old people desperately hold on to life, even when they have wasted most of it away. At least I can say I have lived a life worth living. Some will say maybe even two or three. But now I am near the end, and that's OK. I am ready."

The next morning I was sitting at a cafe, yet again. I had considered my options from every angle, drunk and sober. And I had reached an agreement with myself in both conditions on all counts. It was time. I logged into isawyoumate@gmail.com and typed the subject line: "STEVE HALL IS STILL DEAD", for the avoidance of any doubt. I wrote: "Hi Gunnar. Time flies. I trust you have been busy. This is what I want you to do. Next Thursday, one week from today, I want you to take the 7:33am train from your local station towards the city, carrying the three million in cash in a dark blue Nike sports-bag. Don't sit down. Stand up. During the train-ride someone will approach you and ask for the bag. If that person is hindered in any way, or followed, or if there isn't exactly three million in the bag, there is an email on my PC, addressed to the police and to The World newspaper, set to be sent automatically at 9:30am Thursday. It says: 'Steve Hall. Factory Outlet Centre, Gunnar Fergusen.' Please note, nothing in this email is subject to negotiations."

A Plan

"Have any of you ever heard about being decimated?" Carl, Thor and Vladimir glanced at each other, neither of them answering. Aron was leaning back in his reclining chair as he usually did, arms crossed. It had been a week since they had almost caught Marius, but since then he had disappeared off the face of the earth. He had neither been seen, nor heard from, except for one call to his work and the one to Aron. Not much they could do about that. But what worried Aron much more was that they had yet to uncover Marius' weak spot, something to get him on the hook and reel him in. It seemed like Marius avoided close personal relationships, that he preferred the superficial and uncommitted. Not one of the dozen or so people they had talked to - some voluntarily, others requiring a bit of persuasion - had described Marius as a close friend or relative. Nor did they know if he had any long-term partners. Aron found it worrying. He doubted if Marius would be able to pay back the money, and without a close relative, a sweetheart or a close friend to use as bait he could be difficult to locate. So Aron decided it was time for a motivational lesson.

"Decimation actually means one tenth, the Romans used it on legionaries who didn't perform in battle. The Centurion would line up his soldiers and walk along the ranks, sword in hand, stabbing every tenth man, and if it didn't result in improvements in the next battle, the process would be repeated." Aron lent forward and slammed his fist on the desk, staring each of them down in turn. "You need understand that neither of you are irreplaceable. You are mere foot soldiers. You take orders. If you fail, there are consequences. The little punk owes me three million!" Aron turned red with rage, spitting out the remnants of his lunch as he spoke. "Start again, family, friends, ex girlfriends, anybody, but find something or somebody I can use! What are you waiting for? Get the hell out of here!"

~ ~ ~

It was five minutes to eight. Gunnar was waiting in his office. The latest email had infuriated him. Was the blackmailing crook playing with him? Bossing him around as if he was a little child! He felt humiliated, which also sharpened his senses even more. Not many had been able to get the better of him over the years, whether it was with women, football or business, and he was determined that this self-assured cock-head was not going to either. Joe had called him earlier in the day, saying he'd had a visit from the police. It had taken a while to calm him down. Gunnar was about to pull a hair out of his nose when the doorbell chimed. The coffee was ready.

He reached out his hand in greeting as Peter, Kai and Joe entered, but none of them took it. Gunnar poured coffee and sat down at the head of the table. "I understand these are difficult times, boys. Believe me, I am not doing great myself, not to mention Vivian. We should all expect the police to come calling at some stage. But if we stick to the story of having an evening of crayfish and drinks, which of course we can all confirm, giving us an alibi, there should be no reason for any suspicions being raised. Anything you can add to that, Joe?"

Joe stared at the table. Hesitating, he spoke so softly that the others had to lean forward to hear him: "I actually think it went OK. They told me they'd been through Steve's phone records and he had called me within the last three weeks before his disappearance. I told them the truth, it was about some new computer equipment for his office. They then asked me how well I knew him, if I knew about the threats on Steve's life and if I had any idea what could have happened. There were no questions about where I was Saturday night, nothing about the

Factory Outlet Stores… But I just don't know how long I can keep it up. I think I'll have to take sick leave." He seemed like he had already given up, hunched down, looking pale and weak.

"I'd suggest that's a bad idea", said Gunnar. "It's paramount that we maintain our lives as if nothing has happened. Sick leave could make the investigators prick up their ears."

As usual it was Kai who leapt to Joe's defence. "Can't you see he is falling apart? Have you got no fuckin' empathy? I guess you never did. But isn't it better for Joe to take sick leave than break down completely?"

"What about George Kristoffersen?" Peter interrupted. "Are you certain that he will vote in favour of the Factory Outlet Stores?"

Gunnar was secretly pleased. He knew that if he could persuade Peter, the others would follow. This was a sign that Peter was starting to see things his way. Gunnar looked straight at Peter and said: "Listen, George is Steve's deputy representative, and he will automatically take Steve's place. At least until the next election. Even if the Farmers Party is generally opposed to everything not involving money for farmers, George is in favour of the Factory Outlet development. His sister is hoping to move her BP Service Station there, something I have already said I'd support, and as a politician he will never be taken to task for voting in favour of more jobs for his district. I talked to him a few months ago, and he said straight out that he was in favour, but that Steve was vehemently opposed. Steve was even hoping this would be the issue that could propel him onto the stage of national politics. And even if George was going to baulk at the idea for some reason, I still have the photos of him and Lisa from that party. So, to answer your question, Peter, yes, George is on our side!"

There was a short silence. Gunnar took the print-outs of

the latest email and gave one to each of them. He sipped his coffee while they were all reading, studying their faces. He was still not convinced that neither of them had something to do with the blackmail, but he had decided to let it rest for now.

Kai was the first one to react: "What? In one week? Three days ago it was two." "I know," Gunnar said, "but what can we do? He is pretty clear that nothing is negotiable. I don't know what would happen if we even tried to counter. I don't think we have a choice… How are we going raising the cash, by the way? As for me, I've sold the boat. Luckily I've had someone wanting to buy it for a while, and he turned out to be willing to pay 75% in cash, so that's 1.5 million. I'll have the balance by Monday. What about you guys?"

"Huh? You only got two million for THAT boat?" Kai was incredulous. "That's the price in a buyers market. I asked for two and a half but didn't have much choice as long as he was prepared to pay mostly in cash."

"What if we do nothing?" Peter's question came from left field. Gunnar sipped his coffee to buy some time before responding. "That would be one hell of a chance to take. Maybe one in twenty. Anyone here prepared to risk court, media coverage and prison at that kind of odds? We just don't know who this is, or how he is thinking. How can we NOT pay?"

"We could pretend we never read the email?" Joe ventured without conviction.

"Seriously guys. Wake up. Read it one more time. Does it seem to you like it's coming from someone who'll give up at the first hint of resistance? To me he seems like someone who knows exactly what he wants. I reckon we have no choice. After all you have to spend some to earn some, and none of us will ever come across a project with this kind of financial upside. This is a once in a lifetime opportunity. I for one see this as an investment that we can't afford NOT to make."

"That may be so from your vantage point", Peter said.

"You are much deeper into this than any of us and haven't got a choice, but the rest of us can still get out without too much damage. I haven't decided yet, but I am not prepared to bend over just to save your hide, Gunnar. If I do this, I do it for me. What are your thoughts? Joe? Kai?"

Again, Kai spoke first: "As crazy as it sounds, I have to say I agree with Gunnar. This is the opportunity I have been waiting for all my life. Count me in, and I'll pay my share. We've had a loan application approved to renovate our holiday house, just a matter of paperwork so should have the money Monday or Tuesday at the latest."

Peter turned around to Joe, "What about you? Are you in?"

Joe nodded in agreement, and added, "I've got the money ready."

Gunnar looked at Peter: "Well that leaves you then?"

He knew Peter well, knew that he was as stubborn as himself, and to try to talk him into it would be counter productive. So he didn't say anything else, nor did any of the others. It took quite a while before Peter answered: "Against my better judgement, I'm in, and I've got the money."

Gunnar breathed a quiet sigh of relief and clenched his left hand in victory under the table. If any of them had pulled out, it would have been all over. Even if there were still obstacles to be overcome, it started to seem feasible. "I have a plan", he started calmly, "but there are a few things I need to clarify first. He says that an email is set to be sent automatically at 9:30am. Can that be done?"

Joe answered: "Yes, he's using Gmail. You can write an email, set the date and time to send it, and it will happen. Nothing special."

"Cool", Gunnar said, before addressing Kai: "Do you still have the GPS dongle you used to track Anna with?"

Kai nodded. "Probably needs a new battery."

"And it's the size of twenty kroner coin?"

"Yep, maybe a bit thicker."

"That's OK." Gunnar placed both hands on the table, took

a deep breath and lent forward: "This is what I propose: We put the GPS tracker in the lining of the Nike bag that holds the cash. I have already checked it out, it's easy enough to do. Otherwise we follow the instructions. I'll carry the bag and get on the 7:33 train." Gunnar looked around the table, he was liking what he saw, it was as if they were in the dressing room discussing tactics before a football game. He pointed to Joe: "I want you to get on the train from the station before mine, at 7:28. Being the first station you know you'll be able to find a seat wherever you like. Get into the second carriage looking forward, make sure you look like a normal commuter, wearing a trench-coat and the obligatory briefcase. Make a note of everyone as they enter the train. You've always had an eye for detail and a photographic memory."

"Got it", Joe said, took a pen from his pocket and made some notes on the back of the email print-out.

"Here", Gunnar said as he pushed a blank sheet of paper across the table, "write on that, I'll be shredding those when we have finished."

When Joe had completed his notes, Gunnar continued: "I'll be boarding the same carriage, of course, and unless the train is completely packed, you should be able to see me handing over the bag. If it's full, I'll make sure I stretch my hand and touch the roof as if to steady myself to let you know that the handover has happened. Whenever he exits the train, I want you to follow him as long as you can. If it becomes awkward, just walk past and away. Try to get a glimpse of him, see if he gets into a car, try to get the license plate number, but above all, don't let him see you. His own car is likely either a black Audi or Toyota station wagon. Call us as soon as you are alone. How does that sound, Joe?"

He smiled sheepishly before answering "Yes, except I don't own either a trench-coat or a briefcase." There was a bit of a chuckle around the table, easing some of the tension. "I do, you can borrow mine", Gunnar offered with a grin, before continuing: "Peter and Kai, I need you both in a car, not too far from the end station downtown. Given the way this guy writes, I bet you he is from the west side of Oslo, and he will do this in familiar surroundings. If I am right, he will exit the train downtown or just before and use the morning commuter crowds as a shield. I will call Peter as soon as he gets off the train and then you guys can follow him using the GPS tracker. The point isn't necessarily to get close to him, but to get a photograph of him or of the car. Either way we cannot risk anything until after 9:30. But we have to find out where he is going. If he is feeling safe, he may be going home, or to work. Once we know, we should be able to get him when it suits us."

"What exactly do you mean by 'get him'?" Peter cut to the chase as always. "Have you planned to kill him, too?"

"Hopefully not. We'd have to see. If he is a normal guy with a job and a family, he wouldn't want to be exposed publicly as someone taking advantage of a murder. If we tempt him with a small share of the Factory Outlet Stores, I reckon we can keep him quiet, and return the cash."

"And what if he isn't a normal guy?"

"If so, Peter, then I will take care of it personally. Relax, you won't have blood on your hands. If I am going to get caught for murder, I'll be locked up for quite a while. A second murder won't make too much difference."

"How can you sit here and say things like that?" Again, Joe was about to lose it.

"Firstly, because it's true. That's how it works. And secondly, Joe, please don't have any false illusions about this guy. He is playing with high stakes and is unlikely to be a saint. Instead of reporting a murder he has witnessed, he is taking advantage to enrich himself. He is asking for trouble, and that's what we are going to give him. Maybe even more than he bargained for."

Nobody said anything for quite some time. Joe focused on cleaning dirt from under a finger-nail, Kai was picking at a scar on his elbow, Peter kept turning his wedding ring. A phone rang. They all jumped. Joe answered, listened, he mumbled something illegible before hanging up. "That was my wife. She just heard on the news the police saying that any trace of Steve's mobile had stopped somewhere downtown Oslo last Saturday afternoon. Otherwise the police had nothing new to report on the case."

"And that's as far as they'll get", said Gunnar with conviction. "The only thing they have to go on are the death threats, and that's a dead end."

"But what if the police find those who sent the threats, and they can prove their innocence? Then they'll start looking elsewhere?" Kai looked concerned. "Or worse, they are convicted of the murder. What then, Gunnar?"

"But they won't", said Gunnar with a self-satisfied smile, "because who do you think sent those letters to Steve?" Again, everyone was quiet. They all looked at him quizzically.

Peter was first: "It was you sending those letters?"

"You got it. Well, not all of them. He had already had a few threats, but the last lot came from me. As soon as I realised his engagement in opposing the Factory Outlets development, and how his vote could be decisive, I started thinking that we'd either have to get him on board, or throw him overboard. He got his chance, he was offered a first class ticket, but instead he used the opportunity to use it as a launching pad for a tilt at a national role in politics. At our expense. So I wrote those letters as a kind of insurance policy just in case he turned against us. Which he did."

"I say, Gunnar. I knew you were a cunning bastard, but…" It was obvious Peter was a little impressed.

"But what if the police find that it was you who sent the letters? Then you'll be a suspect anyway?"

"Good thinking, Joe. But that just won't happen. The paper, the envelope, the stamp, everything was handled with gloves on. Printed on a standard printer, posted at the central

GPO. In one of the envelopes I even included a lock of hair from a man standing in front of me at the cash register in the supermarket. The police have more than enough to keep them busy as it is."

They were taking it all in. The mood around the table had changed from anger and disbelief to quiet acceptance of the proposed course of action, exactly as Gunnar had hoped it would.

"OK, boys, let's take five, go for a piss, stretch our legs, before we summarise. I'll put the kettle on."

They all stood up. Joe and Kai headed for the bathroom, Peter followed Gunnar into the kitchen. "You should have been negotiating peace in the middle east. Getting us to agree with you is pure madness. But here we are, having broken our piggy banks, ready to play James Bond. Fuckin' unreal."

"Money, Peter, money. We have all dreamt about being really rich, not reasonably well off kind of rich as we are today, but seriously rich. Now we have the chance, at last. We've all had a bit on the side; maybe some bootleg, some cash work, a double invoice here and there. Neither of us are squeaky clean, let's face it, we haven't been since the eighties, any of us. Not even Joe."

"Joe surprised me a bit, suppose he just ended up in bad company", Peter said with a chuckle. "But, honestly, Gunnar, do you really think we can get the ransom back? A bit far fetched, don't you think?"

"I don't know. Maybe he is a bit like us, and if so it might work. Or he is a real crook and will suffer the consequences. We'll see. Worst case is he'll end up under the rocks, next to Steve."

Kai and Joe came back from the bathroom. They had both splashed water on their faces, looking a bit wet and unkempt. "OK, boys, let's finish up", Gunnar said, grabbing the fresh pot of coffee and returning to the boardroom.

Gunnar poured coffee for everyone, sat down and looked around the table.

"Then we have a plan. What I don't like is that we have no idea who this person is. For all we know it may even be someone we know. So we have to be careful. Finding out who I was wouldn't have been too hard, it happened on a property in my name, from there it was just a matter of Google searches. Question is if he also knows who you are? He knows your first names, except for Peter, but has he managed to connect the dots between us? I am suggesting that you all need to conceal yourselves as much as possible, without looking conspicuous. If he recognises any of you, it's all over. We can't let that happen. Especially you, Joe, as you try to follow him. A trench-coat and a briefcase may not be enough. Give that some thought. Any questions?"

They all looked at each other. Then Kai said: "It appears that Joe has the hardest job. And he is close to breaking point. Maybe we should reconsider our roles?"

"Fair point, Kai. I have been thinking about that, but if we all take a look in the mirror, there is no doubt who stands out the least among us. You are tall, have red hair and are missing a tooth, Peter has his birthmark. If I saw either of you for just a second or two, I would easily remember you. But Joe is kind of ordinary looking, run of the mill. In this instance that's an advantage. Don't take it personally, Joe, it's just the way it is."

"That's OK, Gunnar. I get it." Joe said matter-of-factly.

"Any more questions? ... No? OK, then let's meet back here at 8pm on Tuesday next week. That gives us a day or so before it's going to happen. Everyone bring their share of the cash. Kai's bringing the GPS tracker, don't forget to replace the battery. If anything comes up in the meantime, we stay in touch. Safe trip home, boys."

Gunnar stood up and accompanied them to the front door. They all shook his hand as they walked out.

Man overboard

The sound of a splash woke me up. Maybe because I was sleeping in the aft cabin, close to the waterline. Straight away I realised something was not right. Without thinking, I stumbled out of bed and scrambled up to the wheelhouse. The rain was driving horizontally under a black sky. I stepped outside. The wind howling through the stanchions, the rain hammering the canvas, sharp little waves hitting the side of the boat - all comforting sounds when safely moored as I was. But something, or someone, had hit the water. I walked out to the end of the jetty and stared into the dark sea, dimly lit by the lights of the Marina.

I went back for the searchlight that I knew was always hanging behind the wheelhouse, sweeping it out over the water, the rain making the surface boil. And then I saw something, like a round, pale ball bobbing up and down, 10-15 metre away. That was all I could make out, but I had a fearful inkling that I knew what it was - the bald head of Jon Lauritzen. I dived in, reached out with my hands, but could only feel the water. It was very dark, but I caught a glimpse of the moored boats just behind me and realised I had to swim further out. After a few strokes my fingers hit something, an arm, then the head. He was floating face down and I went under as I tried to turn him over. He was lifeless. I grabbed his collar and mustered all my strength struggling backwards towards the jetty. By the time I got there I had swallowed many mouthfuls of salt-water and was starting to get numb from the freezing cold, battling to hold on. I cried out for help.

I don't know how long I had been lying there, one hand holding onto a piece of rope attached to the jetty, and one hand on Jon's collar, but as I was about to drift into carefree oblivion, I felt a hand grabbing my arm. "H - here," was all I could stutter as I let go. I saw two shadowy figures on their knees grab hold of Jon and pulled him out of the water, dragging him further up the jetty. One of them came back for me, but he couldn't quite grab hold of me and I was too exhausted to be of much help. He put his hands under my arms and stopped me from going under. Then I felt a strong grip around both my wrists and I was finally dragged out of the water.

I was shaking like my whole body was in a cramp, but curiously I wasn't cold, almost the opposite. "You're alive. That's good. Do you live around here?" asked the man with the bear-like grip who had pulled me up. I nodded towards the Island Gypsy. He lifted me up like I was a kid and carried me into the cabin where he removed my wet boxer-shorts, the only thing I had been wearing, and stuffed me into the sleeping bag. He vigorously massaged my body and limbs until I slowly started to regain some feeling and could sense the blood flow returning. I was still shaking, but not as violently as before. "T - t - thanks", I managed to say, and he let go as I curled up into the foetal position.

My saviour found some blankets which he placed over me. "That's the least I can do", he said as he sat down on the bench opposite me. I thought I might have seen him before, maybe at the marina tavern, but we had not met. "C - c - coffee", I said and nodded towards the pantry. He got up to make some, looking like he was comfortable on a boat. As I shakily put the mug to my mouth, I could hear the sirens. I allowed the hot liquid to burn my lips and could feel the warmth as it ran down my throat. I was starting to thaw out. "Is Jon still alive?" I asked.

He looked down, shaking his head slowly: "Don't know, someone started resuscitating him, but it didn't look good. The ambulance is arriving so we'll have to hope for the best. Are you friends?"

"Yeah, I'd say so. As much as you can be friends with

someone you've known for a week. He is something else", I said as I could feel tears welling up. "How about you?" "No, but I do know who he is. People talk, you know." The sirens had stopped.

"What's your name, by the way?" "Marius Tokle. You?" "Garry Larsen. I'm on the catamaran a bit further down. I'll go out and check how things are going. I'll be back." He stood up and left.

I was feeling empty, like a dead battery. Thought of Jon, on what he had said the last time we met. Garry came back after a few minutes, rain running off him. "Sorry, Marius, they tried but he was gone. The ambulance crew declared him dead on arrival... I'll have a cup of coffee, too, if you don't mind." I nodded. "The police are on their way and they'll want to talk to you, of course. What did happen?"

I sat up in the sleeping bag, leaning against the side of the boat, tried to recapitulate: "Not quite sure. I woke up from hearing a splash. Went outside and saw someone floating in the water. So I just dived in. But why, or how he fell in, I have no idea."

We sat there for a little while, staring into our coffee. Finally Garry said: "You are a hero for what you did, Marius. You could easily have drowned yourself. Just saying."

"Yeah, maybe ... thanks for that ... I don't know, just had to dive in."

Garry stood up, looking a bit sheepish: "Hope it's OK, but I'll get back to my boat. Need to get some more sleep before I go to work."

"Of course, Garry, no worries. I'm OK. Thanks so much again. Can I stop by later?"

"Sure. I'll be back around seven." He smiled and left.

I laid back down, closed my eyes and was almost asleep when I jolted, looked at my watch: 2:50am. It was Thursday already and in five hours I was due to meet Gunnar.

Somebody was gently shaking me awake. A drenched policeman was standing over me. "Are you Marius Tokle?" His soft, almost feminine, voice was in stark contrast to what looked like a rather well built man. "Yes, that's me, I said, swallowing a yawn."

"Do you have any form of identification, please?" The contrast between voice and the physical appearance was startling, almost made me laugh, but I contained myself. Except for the feeling of two cold claws in my back I had regained normal body heat. "Yes, I do", I said as I unzipped the sleeping bag, "but allow me to get dressed first." I had one clean pair of underpants left. I put on two t-shirts, another shirt and my hooded sweater, pants and doubled up on the socks, too. "I need coffee", I said looking at the constable, "would you like one?" He said yes, please. I got my wallet out and gave him my photo ID. He looked at the photo: "Marius Tokle, born October 24th, 1984."

"That's me."

"I don't know if you know, but the person you tried to rescue, Jon Lauritzen, he is deceased. Hence, we are treating this as a suspected homicide. Can you tell me what happened?"

And I did as best as I could with all the details I could remember. When I was finished we both sat there, each with a cup of coffee keeping us warm, his little notebook on the table.

"How long did it take from hearing the splash until you were outside?" "It can't have been long, ten - fifteen seconds at the most."

"And you couldn't see anyone else out there?"

"No, nobody … You're thinking if somebody had pushed him? I don't think so. I think I would have heard or sensed it when I came outside."

"Did you know him well?" he asked tentatively, as if we were two friends having a private conversation.

"No, I had only known him for a week. But we had a bit of contact over the last few days. He was an interesting man. Witty. Engaging." I could feel the tears, but pushed them back.

"Do you have any idea how it happened?"

His gaze more alert this time. I didn't quite know how I could be giving anything away, but I became more wary. I couldn't afford for any of this to impact on the arrangements I had already made with Gunnar. And with Aron.

"No idea. But I'd be guessing you'll find alcohol in his blood. He was fond of a glass, or two or three. What he was doing outside in this weather, I do not know, but the jetty is unstable, it's easy to lose your balance."

He made more notes. Then there was a knock on the hull. "Please come in", I said automatically, expecting another policeman. It turned out to be a dripping wet policewoman, more woman than police in my estimation. She was stunning; dark, long auburn hair, large brown eyes and full lips.

Under the shapeless uniform I could detect curves and tight muscles. I was suddenly aware of my own appearance, hair ruffled, a scruffy beard, wearing a hooded jacket. If I looked like the way I felt I didn't stand a chance. I offered her a coffee, which she declined.

"We are almost done", the policeman said. "Do you have anything to add?"

I was thinking of what Jon had told me a couple of days earlier and decided to tell them. Jon was dead, anyway. "Well, one thing, Jon did tell me that he was happy with how he had lived his life, but that it was coming to an end, and he was OK with that. But it didn't occur to me that he'd top himself. He didn't appear depressed. But now, all things considered… Maybe … I don't know."

The policeman took some more notes. I couldn't help but look at his colleague. What an odd team - couldn't stop looking at her, nor listening to his voice. What sort of good cop, bad cop routine they'd be playing at was beyond me. Unfortunately, although I doubted what followed next was intentional. The effect was nevertheless that I was caught off guard, when out of nothing, she asked, "Is this your boat?"

"Well, yes, no. It's not my boat." The policeman looked up

from his notes.

"I am looking after it for a mate, Brad Brown. He is sailing in the Caribbean this winter and asked me to look after it. I am redecorating my apartment so I am living here temporarily."

"Are you doing the redecorating yourself?" she said looking at me in a way that under different circumstances I would have found flirtatious.

"Yes, pretty much", I said with some pride, as if I was an accomplished handyman.

"Strange. Normally people that do that have scratches and remnants of paint on their hands." A hint of suspicion in her voice, her well coiffed eyebrows narrowing.

"Haven't got started, yet. Just prepping and getting the supplies together." I could hear myself saying it just a tad too fast. Why had I moved here already if the renovations hadn't started yet? They both looked at me with some suspicion. She continued, her voice now a bit more business-like: "So is there anyone we can contact to verify that you have permission to stay on the boat? We do hear of homeless people moving into boats during winter without the owner's knowledge."

"Jon Lauritzen did know, but that's no good now. You can try to call Brad, although I don't know if you'll get hold of him. I've got his number on my mobile." And as soon as I said it I remembered that the SIM card was in my wallet. A non-issue was fast becoming tricky. But I didn't have a choice. I had to continue. As I reached for my wallet, I said: "I have had problems with my mobile. Think there is something wrong with the SIM card. Let me give it a try." I removed the cover of my mobile and inserted the SIM. It came to life and I entered my PIN code. "Seems like it's working now ... Let's see, Brad's number is 9249-5551." I swallowed and forced a smile. The policeman made notes.

"Well, I reckon that's it for now, but you'll have to come in for a formal interview later. Please leave your mobile on, so we can get hold of you. Will you remain here, or will you move back to your apartment?"

"I'll likely stay here until the renovations are finished."

"OK then, that's it for now. Thanks for the coffee", he said as he stood up and reached out his hand. I shook his hand and nodded, before they both disappeared up the stairs and out. This didn't go to plan, caught in one lie after another, obviously guilty of something, worst case suspected of murder.

I put my head in my hands and felt like squealing - like a drowning cat.

~ ~ ~

Aron woke from his mobile vibrating its way across his bedside table, like a lemming heading towards the cliff. He was a sound sleeper, something he liked to attribute to a clean conscience, but he still woke up within seconds. He looked at the clock, 3:31am, whoever it was ought to have a pretty good reason. He picked up the phone and answered: "This better be important, Carl." Carl explained that Marius had activated his mobile and that their Telco contact was on his way to the ops centre to triangulate the signal. The only thing he knew at this stage was that the signal was coming from the bay area near town. "OK. Get the boys and head there." Then he hung up.

He had almost gone back to sleep when it vibrated again. Carl again. "Yes?" he inquired. Carl told him that one of the guys had been listening in on the police frequency and heard that a certain Marius Tokle had been involved in a drowning accident at the King's Marina, and that a constable had requested a background check on him and the registered owner of a boat with the license number AAZ371. "Get over there. I am on my way," Aron said and jumped out of bed, surprisingly agile for someone weighing close to 200 kilos.

~ ~ ~

I went up to the wheelhouse and looked out. It was 3:44am. Through the rain I could see the police-car was still at the entrance. What were they talking about? Did they really think that I had pushed Jon? Were they going to arrest me and interrogate me further? It would be rather inconvenient considering I was due to meet Gunnar within a few hours. There was also no way I'd postpone. Every day that passed increased the risk that the police would get to Gunnar. I had to get away as soon as possible. Then I could turn myself into the police once my business with Gunnar and Aron had been settled.

I packed my laptop, keys, wallet, mobile. Shit! The mobile was still on. Had been for about fifteen minutes. I had received 32 text messages. They would have to wait. I turned it off and removed the SIM card. Rolled everything into a cotton sweater and stashed it all into a water-proof bag, put on a Gore-Tex jacket and a cap and went back up. The police-car was still there, blocking my only exit. If they were to come back right now, I'd be unable to get away. That is, unless...

Jon kept a tiny, grey plastic dinghy right under the bow of his Fairline. It was the only option. I could row across to the other side of the bay, get ashore there and then make my way back to where my car was. Under the cover of darkness and in this weather nobody would even see me. The police-car was still there. If I waited to see if anybody would come for me, it could be too late. So I pulled the hood down as far it would go and stepped onto the jetty.

The wind was still fierce, and I had to brace myself. The little dinghy was neatly tied up, halfway under the jetty and half full of water. I dropped my water-proof bag down and lowered myself into the dinghy, immediately soaked up to my ankles. I untied it and pushed off so I was completely covered by the underside of the jetty above. If possible, it was even darker under there so I had to feel my way between the concrete poles. Something hard hit my knee. I winced and reached out to find an iron bar protruding. I tied the dinghy to it and felt a bit safer. Slowly and methodically I began bailing.

After a few minutes I started thinking that I may have overreacted. Why cross the bay if the police had left? Maybe they were just sitting there discussing things before leaving. Or maybe they were taking the opportunity for a bit of smooching? That's what I would have done given half a chance. I decided to make my way back to my boat and check if the police-car was still there.

But just as I pushed off I heard footsteps above. Someone was walking, no, running towards my boat. Then came another. I kept as still as I could. I heard one of them cry out: "Carl, here it is, AAZ371." He was standing almost directly above me, I could see the soles of his shoes. Then there were three of them. "Vladimir, go back and make sure he can't leave the jetty. Thor, wait here and cover any exits off the boat. I'll step aboard."

I kept as still as I could, given that I was in a small dinghy, I was getting very cold again, and started shaking. This was not the police. There had been two of them, and their names were definitely not Thor, Carl or Vladimir. And if it wasn't the police, it would have to be Aron's men. And as long as one of them was standing right above me I didn't dare trying to get away. After a few minutes in an impossibly awkward position I just had to change my grip. I did, and was relieved there was no reaction above. I stayed put. The one who had entered the boat came out. "He is fuckin' not here. I have been through the boat from bow to stern, checked every compartment, turned it upside down. He is just not there the little bastard. Just like the other day. Vanished. The punk is getting on my nerves in a bad way!"

"Not to mention for Aron. He'll go nuts."

"Shut up, Thor, give me the torch. Maybe he has taken shelter in one of the other boats. As long as Vladimir is standing at the entrance he won't get out. You stay here."

Just what I didn't need - Aron's henchmen. I just had to get away. My night vision had improved somewhat, I could make out the shadows between the poles, so I started pulling myself out towards the end of the jetty. The further I got, the waves got a bit sharper and the wind started pulling at the dinghy, too. A couple of times I had to drop down on all fours to avoid capsizing.

I had made my way almost to the end, where the venerable 'King's Boathouse' was still standing proud above. The sweep of a torch light almost hit the dinghy, but I kept going. The next sweep skirted the side of the boat but it didn't stop, and the next time I was hidden behind a pole. I held on for dear life, but the pole was wide and slippery and I had to let go and found myself in between two poles, felt like a deer in the headlights on a motorway, helplessly waiting to be hit. But it didn't happen. I could see several torches in the vicinity of the Island Gypsy. I either had to stay where I was under the shelter of the jetty, or I had to start rowing across the bay.

After a few moments hesitation I grabbed the oars, but by now my fingers were so numb I couldn't grip properly at first. And by the time I could, I was already in open water, drifting back to the main jetty. If I continued I would be seen, so I put my back to the front and the bow into the wind and the waves, rowing as if my life depended on it. Which it did. Away from the shelter of the jetty the waves were angrily slapping at my back for every stroke, I was making some headway, but it was slow going, and a couple of times an oar would slip and I'd be going backwards with the wind.

In the end I had no choice, it was do or die. So I turned the dinghy away from the wind, the only way I could get over to the other side of the bay. I was gathering speed with the waves when a sweep of a torch hit me. The light beam was weak, and by the time it came back I had managed to hunch down into the dinghy. I let the dinghy drift sideways with the wind and the waves for a while, at times dangerously close to rolling over. When I dared look up next, the light beams seemed a safe distance away. Had they seen me? I felt certain that they had seen the dinghy, but probably not me, and in this weather a dinghy having broken its moorings was not so unusual. Either way, I had to get to the other side, so again I took the oars with my frozen fingers, and after ten or twelve desperate strokes across the waves I hit rocks. I grabbed my bag, got out of the dinghy and waded ashore. My legs were barely holding me and I was shaking like a rag-doll in the mouth of a manic dog.

~ ~ ~

Aron had arrived and he and Carl had found shelter in the wheelhouse of the Island Gypsy while Thor checked every boat with a torch and Vladimir kept covering the exit. "When we arrived", Carl started, "the cop car was just leaving. As far as I could see, given the shit weather, there were two cops in the front and nobody in the back. Thor and Vladimir saw the same. 30 seconds later we were on the jetty, and since then Vladimir has been standing at the exit. He either left before the cops did, or he is still out here somewhere."

Aron was standing at the wheel, peering out as if manoeuvring through unknown waters. He disliked intensely this situation with Marius. He could like playing cat and mouse, but only if he was the cat. This was the other way around. Suddenly a beam of light hit them and they could see Thor running towards them and came inside.

"Think I might've seen him", he gasped, as if just surfacing for air.

"Where?" Carl grabbed his arm.

"Out there." Thor had to draw breath a couple of times before he could continue. "A boat, a dinghy, drifting with the waves. The beam was almost out of reach so I can't be sure if there was anyone in it, but I think so." Thor was about to open the door to point to where it was, when a loud crack was heard. Aron just stood there, with one half of the wooden wheel of the Island Gypsy in each hand.

"You two get across to the other side. Get hold of a dozen more guys with torches and cover all the exits from the peninsula. Vladimir stays where he is, I will stay here. Keep me posted, and whatever you do, don't come back empty handed!"

~ ~ ~

After having walked straight into a rock wall, the remnants of the old breakwater most likely, I was standing on solid ground again, on a gravel road. I had been to the other side of the peninsula before, an area with many public areas, including several museums and what was Oslo's most popular 'beach', but this side was unfamiliar to me, consisting of old mansions inhabited by some of the old monied elite of Oslo. I started shuffling along the gravel towards the main thoroughfare not too far away. My shoes gurgling for every step, my clothes so soaked and heavy they were more of a hindrance, but I was too tired to do anything about it. Had they seen me in the dinghy or not?

The gravel road came to a fork. My objective was to get to my car, remove my clothes and start the heater, drive around naked with the seat warmers on high until I was due to meet with Gunnar. I kept to the right, pretty sure I was heading the right way. I soon started seeing the lights from the road and I knew where I was. It gave me some extra strength and I was almost jogging when a car came towards me and I spotted two silhouettes in its headlights. Who in their right mind would be out for a walk in this weather this time of night? I panicked and jumped to the side of the road, up an embankment. But it was quite steep, and I fell, every time I tried to get up I slid back down. After a few attempts I just laid down, a couple of metre from the side of the road. My heart was beating like a drum, and my breath stuck in my throat. Face down in the mud, I didn't see them passing me, but felt it, like a couple of 'death eaters' from Harry Potter.

When I was absolutely certain they had passed, I stood up. Listened. All I could hear was the wind and the rain. I got back out on the road. Ahead of me was a roundabout, and a car parked on the wrong side of the road. Lights on. A checkpoint, no doubt. Aron's men had seen me, and now they were trying to block my exit from the peninsula.

I looked at my watch. In two hours I would have to be ready for Gunnar. No more time to lose. Even if Aron now controlled the only access road, there were other options. On foot and taking me further away from my car. Most likely they'd have lookouts on those paths, too. It was starting to look like a game of chess. I couldn't go straight ahead, not right, nor left, the only way was back to where I came from, straight into the clutches of Aron. Check mate.

Hopelessness was starting to take over, what little warmth I had regained was lost again, and time was running out. And just then, on this dark and miserable night, alone on a deserted road with nowhere to go, I started thinking about John Maynard Keynes. As you do. I had already forgotten most things I once learnt in Business School, except Keynes, the economist credited with returning America to prosperity after the crash of '29. His philosophy was to do the opposite of everyone else. When investors yelled out their sell orders, he would buy, and vice versa. He made a lot of money that way. No doubt I had been observed rowing across the bay. The last thing Aron would expect was that I'd go back the same way. Consequently there was no reason for him to stay with the boat. He was more likely sitting in that car. So that's what I had to do, get back to the dinghy and back to the Marina.

Decision made, the head was willing, but the legs were

not. Slowly, like an old man shuffling down a hospital corridor, I started retracing my steps. I could see torches flickering across a field to my right, but it didn't concern me anymore. I was focused on my mission. For a while I thought I was lost until I got back to the fork and the gravel road. From there I found my way back to the rock wall where the dinghy was still banging about in the shallow water. I threw my bag in and pushed the boat in front of me as I waded out until the water was up to my hips, then I sort of rolled into it, my head hit the seat plank, but I hardly noticed it. The thought that I was about to outsmart Aron gave me a perverse sense of satisfaction that eased both the pain and the cold, even allaying my fear.

I rowed into the wind for a while under the cover of the land until I got to a point where I estimated there was no more than a couple of hundred metre back across to my marina. I sat up straight, getting ready to use what strength I had left, got a good foothold and turned the boat 45 degrees, dipping both oars deep in the water to get maximum purchase against the waves. Unfortunately, as soon as I hit the first large wave one of the oars slipped out of the rowlock and then slipped out of my hand and was swallowed by the sea. The waves were throwing the dinghy about like a cork. I kept rowing feverishly with the oar I had left but realised I had no steering so just had to get across somehow, to wherever I landed on the other side. I was so focused on keeping the dinghy afloat and moving that I didn't realise where I was until I literally hit a floating jetty. The initial shock quickly replaced by relief, I manoeuvred the dinghy into an empty berth, grabbed my bag and crawled out.

I didn't know exactly where I was, but through the rain I could see the lights from the main road, so I realised I had landed at one of the small private marinas at the bottom of the bay. Question now was, run like a dog, or sneak out like a feline? I wanted the former, but chose the latter. I lurked towards the gate, seeking shelter from the moored boats that had still not been taken out for winter storage. The gate was of course locked and surrounded by barbed wire on both sides, so I just jumped in. After all, I couldn't get any colder or wetter than I already was. It turned out it was quite shallow and soon I found myself back on land yet again.

How I managed to get from there to my car, a distance of a kilometre or so, I'll never quite know. What I do recall, is that when I was standing next to my car, my fingers on my right hand were clutching my bag and were so numb I couldn't get them loose. And when I did, there was no way I could unzip the bag. My fingers were just too numb. After everything that had happened I was standing less than a metre from relative safety and the promise of warmth, but I was unable to open my bag to get my keys out. I tried blowing on my hands to no avail. A car, a taxi, was coming towards me and I just got out and stood in front of it. It screeched to a halt but didn't quite manage to stop so there I was, bent over the bonnet, sliding slowly to one side as the driver got out. "What are you doing? Are you crazy?" He grabbed my arm and helped me back on my feet. I gesticulated towards my bag now on the ground and stammered: "Can you please open it." He looked at me like I had just fallen out of the sky with the rain. "Please", I said, holding out my stiff, frozen fingers in front of me.

He picked up the bag, still looking confused at me. I nodded, tried to smile. He pulled the zipper open, and I held my hands out so he could give me the bag which he did a bit like it was a religious offering. I staggered back to my car, rummaged around in the bag until I found the keys and could push the door button. I opened the door and more or less fell into the front seat, put the key in the ignition and started the car, started the heater, turned on the seat warmer. Heaven was near. And it was 5:17am, in less than an hour I had to be ready to meet Gunnar.

The Handover

I had been standing in the same spot for fifteen minutes. It was 6:53am, still no sign of Gunnar, and in less than half an hour he was due to catch the train. During morning rush hour it would take him at least fifteen minutes to drive to the station and park his car. But his car was still here. Maybe he had caught a cab earlier? Unlikely.

On the way there I had stopped at a convenience store and bought four hotdogs and a cup of coffee. The store attendant had started laughing when I entered, he even asked if he could twist me dry, but he apologised as I approached the counter and asked me what happened. He pointed out that I had a protruding and bloodied cut on my forehead and gave me a large handful of tissues to wipe the blood and dirt off my face. I put a couple of large bills on the counter, waved away the change, devoured the hotdogs, put both hands gratefully around the steaming hot coffee cup and got back into my car.

This was not the way I had envisaged the handover - cutting it fine for time, wet, cold and exhausted. Fortunately, I had planned everything meticulously. Gunnar and Vivian lived in an old villa renovated and converted to four luxury units. On one of my surveying trips the previous Saturday I had noticed a "For Sale" sign on one of the other units, so I attended an open for inspection that same afternoon. The unit was of a high standard, officially valued at 8.5 million, although no off street parking. Gunnar's car was a Mercedes E-class Estate, which had been parked in the same spot every one of the four times I had been there. Two houses further down, next to a small coppice of fir trees, there was a narrow track, not marked on any maps; just a local short-cut up the hill to the next road, including a convenient set of steps at the last steep bit. From Gunnar's house to where I had parked was a six minute quick walk. Exactly. I was wearing my hooded sweater and also carried a replica pistol. I had bought it on a whim, not sure if I would need it.

7am. I was hiding behind the garbage shed next door. The heavy rain had subsided, not that it made much of a difference. In 33 minutes Gunnar was due to catch the train. He should be coming out soon.

A couple more minutes passed, the front door opening, and I moved the few metre to a position behind Gunnar's car, kneeling, holding onto the rear bumper, the hood concealing my face, the pistol in the other hand, suddenly unsure if I'd be able to stand up again. Tried to breathe calmly, achieving the opposite. The point of no return. This was serious. I counted, ready to pounce as soon as Gunnar opened his car door. But it was taking too long. I peered out from behind the car and saw another pulling out from the kerb. False alarm. I considered getting back behind the shed but stayed put, it was now or never.

Then I heard a door close, steps approaching, the click of the remote and the orange indicator of the Mercedes blinking right in my face. I waited until I could hear the car door opening, staggered up like a new-born foal, and grabbed the door just as it was about to close. The man, it had to be Gunnar, tried pushing me away, but I had managed to put my body between the door and the frame. All I said was: "Gunnar. The money." My voice sounded strange; harsh and throaty. He leaned towards me, tried to twist around so he could see me, tried grabbing my arm. It was Gunnar alright. He looked like somebody had just hit him. "Give me the Nike bag", I screamed right into his ear. I tried to wrest away from him, but he held on. It was only when I started waving the pistol that he let go. The bag was in his lap. I grabbed it, felt the weight, five - six kilos. I took a couple of steps away from the car. "Drive to the station!" I commanded before slamming the door shut.

Nothing happened. He was just sitting there, staring at me. I pointed the pistol at him. Still no movement. In desperation I banged the grip of the gun into the side window. That worked. The glass went milky white. He turned the ignition, the lights went on, pulled out and started driving. Twenty metre down the road he stopped. I strode towards the car, the pistol held out in front of me. When I was almost by the car he continued driving. I waited until the car disappeared around the corner.

Gunnar stopped the car. He was shaking with anger, slapping both hands on the wheel. Should he turn around? He grabbed his mobile. Before Peter could even answer it poured out of him: "Fucking hell, he tricked us! He's had us totally fooled!" Stressed out, Gunnar explained what had happened, when Kai interrupted, "I've got him on the GPS. He is moving north, between some houses and a row of units."

"Great", Gunnar exclaimed, "I know where he is, I'll drive to where that road comes out, you guys go to the other end, near the sports ground. We've got him cornered. Maybe this was better after all. I'll call Joe, then I'll call you back." Gunnar could feel the adrenalin of the hunt. Senses sharpened, as he spun the car around.

I was staggering up the track. It was wet and slippery. I had face planted twice already. Hands on thighs getting up the steep parts. I could feel the bag that I had thrown over my shoulder slapping my lower back for every step. Was it too heavy? Or to light? Hadn't given myself time to check it. Hopefully it contained three million. How absurd it was that I couldn't keep it! I was approaching where I had parked my own car; a few more steps, I'd have to jump a fence, get through a small apple orchard, then I was there. Without the four hotdogs for extra energy I wouldn't have been able to make it.

At that moment I was overcome with a combination of elation and relief, as if I had just climbed the highest mountain.

Removing my clothes I just lost it, tears running, and I ended up on all fours, convulsing like a baby, releasing pent-up emotions without inhibitions. Spent, I finally stood up, suddenly light as a feather, reached up and looked up towards the early dawn sky, glimpses of light grey between the breaking storm-clouds. I was Rocky. I was Braveheart. I was a winner. Leaving the clothes on the ground, I grabbed my keys, pressed through some shrubbery, covering the crown jewels with the bag in front of me, walked to the car, patted the roof before getting in, the leather immediately stuck to my naked butt.

~ ~ ~

"He has stopped!", Kai exclaimed, sounding like a kid playing spin the bottle.

"Are you able to see if he has entered a house, or is he on the road? Wouldn't surprise me if he lived in the neighbourhood." Gunnar detested being conned like this. It stuck to his craw and he would never give up until he had his revenge. With interest. The blackmailer being a neighbour wouldn't help the situation.

"He is on the road. Most likely in a car. The GPS is accurate to within a few metre."

"OK. That sounds right. Then he can go either east or west." Gunnar was thinking as hard as he could. This guy was unpredictable so they would have to think outside the square, too. He had an idea, maybe he is on his way to the train station near the Holmenkollen Ski Jump? That's only a few hundred metre as the crow flies. Maybe he is just resting. He was soaked. Maybe he has a bag with dry clothes up there?"

"Sure, that's a possibility", Kai said, "but if he has a car, why is he taking the train?"

"I don't know, just want to keep all the options open. He has tricked us once already. No fuckin' way I'll let him do it twice!"

~ ~ ~

I put the Nike bag in my lap and unzipped it. Slowly; put my hand inside, it certainly felt like money. I tipped the bag onto the side on the passenger seat, bunches of 1000 kroner bills with strings around them. I counted one, 50.000. I counted the number of bunches. 60. Looked like mostly unused bills. Three million. The feeling of elation returned, like a wet dream just before you wake up. I felt free. Free from Aron, free from Gunnar, even free from myself.

~ ~ ~

"He is on the move", Kai almost yelled into the mobile, "going east … fast … so he must be driving."

"Awesome", Gunnar replied, equally eager. "He is coming towards you. Stay there. I'll stay out of sight, don't want him to recognise my car. See if you can get behind him, so you can get the registration number."

"Yes, he is coming towards us."

"Perfect, right into the lion's den. There are more cars about than usual this morning. Probably because of the bad weather, but he should be there in five minutes." Gunnar winced. He wasn't so sure they'd come to an 'arrangement' as he had suggested. The risk was just too great. If he had managed to kill Steve, a friend, then surely he'd be able to kill a total stranger!

"He has stopped. Maybe just traffic?"

"Possibly. Why else would he have stopped? There is nothing along that road, only houses. Give him a few seconds." Gunnar was pretty confident. Maybe a tree had fallen over during the night, blocking the road, but besides that, there was no doubt the guy was on his way towards them."

"Still no movement", Kai said. Then silence. Hearing a pin drop kind of silence. Common sense dictated movement any time now, but nothing happened.

Gunnar was the first to open his mouth: "Something is not

right. If it was just traffic, it would have moved by now. Maybe he has parked? Or crashed?"

"Impossible to say", Kai responded, "but the pointer hasn't moved. What do we do now?"

"Drive towards him. I will, too." Gunnar's enthusiasm had disappeared. "Tell me what's happening. Lots of traffic?"

"Nope, no cars at all so far, but the road is quite narrow, cars parked on both sides." A short while after, Kai continued: "A black BMW, behind that is a green Land Rover."

"Make a note of all the registration numbers that you see."

"Of course", Kai said, sounding slightly annoyed, what did Gunnar think he was?

"Another BMW, white. But no sign of a traffic jam. Something must have happened."

"That's what I'm afraid of, but I still don't get what it is. How far away are you?"

"Not far, two more bends."

Gunnar's hands was so tight on the wheel his knuckles were white as ivory. He barked: "What's happening?"

"Wait, wait, just around the next bend!" A few more seconds went by, "Nothing. Nothing at all."

"What the fuck do you mean, nothing?"

"Exactly what I am saying, Gunnar. Nothing! We are right on the spot where the pointer is blinking, but there is nothing here. No cars. No people."

"Could there be something wrong with the tracking device? Maybe it has stalled somehow?"

"Nope, it's sending signals, it's blinking, so it's working. I'll get out and have a look."

Another car passed them, a VW Golf. Kai started walking back and forth along the side of the road, searching. It didn't take long, in the gravel just below the edge of the paved road, a black Nike bag, open and empty.

~ ~ ~

Sound of a Murder

I started the car. Revved the engine. Felt the vibrations through my body. The sun still low in the sky and it was overcast, so nobody would see me being naked inside the car. The time was 7:42am. I started driving down the road. I scrambled around to find the checklist I had written up, just to be sure: 1, Car keys, hood, pistol; 2, Swap bags; 3, Delete the email before 9:30. Was it paranoid to think Gunnar had planted a GPS tracker in the bag, or was it naive to think that he had not? Either way, it would be stupid to take that risk. With one hand on the wheel, I put the money in the other bag I had brought with me, opened the window and threw out the Nike bag. Then I turned the car around. If he was tracking me, I wasn't going to make it easy for him.

I drove around at random for a while. It was still raining, but by now my car was toasty, the seat warmers almost singing my skin. I got to the ring-road during peak hour, it was slow going, and by now it was daylight. A truck driver towering above hooted his horn and grinned down at my nakedness. I gave him the thumbs up, my short career as a flasher revealed. By now I was on my way out towards the industrial district, traffic flowing more freely. I turned on the radio, it was playing 'You can leave your hat on' by Joe Cocker. When it finished, a chirpy announcer came on: "Well that was the song 'You can leave your hat on', but apparently not so for a driver spotted stark naked in his car on his way to work. Maybe he forgot to get dressed, or he's got the wrong day, either way, we wish him all the best!"

That made me snap out of it, bursted my bubble. Here I was, with three million in cash, driving on one of the busiest roads in Norway, naked. If the police stopped me now, I would have some explaining to do, not just the nakedness and the money, but above all the connection to the late Jon Lauritzen! It was time to get real, I grabbed my sweater from the dry bag in the back seat. It was 8:38. It gave me 50 minutes to delete the email before it would send. That should work.

I drove for another half hour to a quiet parking lot near the alpine skiing centre outside of Oslo. Except for an old, abandoned van, it was empty. I counted the money once more. It was all there. The time was 9:16. I was thinking of Gunnar, that I had used a killer to help me pay my own criminal debt. It was surreal. But maybe no more surreal than being chased by thugs, and even more the possibility of being a murder suspect. But with a bit of luck it would be sorted out by the end of the day, like the morning fog yielding to the sun. The first step was to delete the email before it would go to the police and to 'The World' newspaper. I did consider sending it anyway. Gunnar was a murderer, and I did not feel any moral obligation to honour our agreement. But the police would still want to know who was behind the isawyoumate@gmail.com email address, and maybe even able to find out. Even Google can be subpoenaed. Hence, self-interest took precedence so I decided to delete it.

I turned on my laptop and connected to the Internet. 63 emails came flowing into my private mail-box. I realised that Aron could track me down again, but I didn't think it mattered any more. Now that I had the money.

Instead of driving back to Oslo, I kept going north through the many small towns looking for somewhere to buy some clothes to wear. After all, I was still naked from the waist down. I finally found a shopping centre around 10am, just as it was about to open. I parked the car, turned on my laptop for a quick search and found the number of a menswear shop at the centre. I found my mobile, took the SIM card from my wallet and installed it. I rang and introduced myself with the enthusiasm of an insurance salesman: "Hi, my name is Trond, and I am sitting in a black Audi A4 station wagon in the parking lot. The problem is that I am almost naked. Long story, but just say that I am getting married soon and my mates took me out for a bucks night that went a bit out of control. Get the picture?"

She chuckled at the other end of the phone, saying yes, she got it, and how could I help, audibly chewing gum. "Well, I need a pair of pants, underwear, socks, a belt, t-shirt, a long-sleeved shirt and a sweater. If you could ring that up, and come out to the parking lot, I'll give you an extra thousand for the trouble."

Sure, she said, giggling, but I am on my own so will need to get some help from the shoe-store next door. "Ah, yes, I need shoes, too. Size 43. I am 25 years old. Six foot tall. Size large."

After about 15 minutes I saw her coming out, a frumpy looking young girl, walking towards me in the almost empty car-park. I rolled down the window and waved, "Fantastic, thanks so much, don't be afraid I've covered up as best as I can." She stopped smiling and backed off a bit when she saw me close up, still dirty and bloodied as I was. I calmed her down, explaining how my mates had left me out in the woods, drunk as a skunk, having to solve a bunch of cryptic clues to find my way back to my car. It had taken me two days, I told her.

She stared at me with eyes wide open not sure whether to believe me or not, chewing away. I took a 1,000 kroner note and handed it to her. "This is for you. You've saved my day. Really cute you are, too!" I gave her my most charming smile. She lit up and relaxed, I was guessing more from the flattery than the money, and handed me the bags with the clothes. "That'll be 1,398 for the clothes and 399 for the shoes. The pants, socks and sweater were on sale. Hope it all fits." I gave her another 2,000 and said for her to keep the change. She almost curtsied as she took the money and traipsed happily back to the store, reminding me of a hippo in a skirt from a cartoon I remembered seeing many years ago.

I continued driving north. Stopped at a road rest stop and

put the clothes on. They were a good fit, albeit not quite my style. But how could I expect more, having just purchased a whole outfit for the cost of a good pair of branded jeans? I turned right towards the freeway heading back to Oslo, made a couple more detours on the way just to see if anyone was following me. I needed a shower, a soft bed and a very long sleep. I had the money if Aron happened to be waiting for me, even if it wasn't due for another week. I almost hoped he'd be there, just to see his face as I put the money on the table.

Blackout

The inevitable reaction to the last 24 hours of drama came as I was driving back towards Oslo; first through the endless expanse of green forest, then onto the freeway. By the time I was passing the Oslo Airport exit it was mainly the seatbelt keeping me upright, eyes heavy, mind numb, and on more than one occasion I was woken by the sound of the tyres crossing the road marking as I drifted across to the other lane, once or twice by the angry bleat from a car about to overtake. Common sense would have me pull over for a power-nap, but I was so desperate to get home to my own bed that I kept going.

I kept on hitting my face, slapping my thighs, even a failed attempt at pocket pinball, all in the interest of staying awake. And somehow, more or less on auto-pilot, I finally found myself pulling up outside my apartment block, grabbed my bags, staggered to the front door and up the stairs to the second floor; hands shaking as I just about managed to unlock the door, dropped everything, fell onto my bed, face down, dead to the world even before the mattress had stopped undulating.

I thought I was still dreaming when the cold water hit me and started running down my neck and face. In the background I could hear droning voices, like listening to the surf breaking in the distance. Unpleasant, but still just a dream. Someone was laughing … I retreated back into dreamland … Another wave hit me, this one more like acid, burning my neck and back and down the arms. I rolled over, tried to get rid of it. As I opened my eyes I was looking straight at the gorilla, I had just escaped a couple of weeks earlier. He had a vicious smirk on his face and a steaming bucket in his hand. At the end of the bed I could see Aron, straddling a pegged wooden dining chair, looking relaxed, as if visiting an old aunt in hospital.

"What the fuck is this?" I yelled out as I sat up and retreated until I hit the back of the bed, scared shitless.

"Nothing to worry about, Marius", Aron said, "just a bit of water, the cold didn't work so we tried hot instead." The bag with the money was hanging over the back of the chair.

"Well, there is your money. Take it and get out. We're even." I put my hand on my neck, it felt like I was badly sunburnt.

"That's not quite right, Marius. Financially, you are right, and to be honest I didn't think you'd deliver, I'll give you that", he said admiringly, like a proud dad. And then he leaned forward, cocked his neck like a boxer entering the ring getting ready to fight, and asked with feigned curiosity and more than a hint of menace: "But what about consequential damages, Marius? Last night I was woken up at 3:30. For the last couple of weeks I've had a small army of my cohorts on full alert just because you were hiding. You turned off your mobile against my very clear order. In addition, I have my reputation to consider. It's like my brand, and it needs protection. I can't be seen to be hoodwinked by a rank amateur!"

"What the hell are you talking about? You've got the money as agreed, even before it was due, and with twice the interest. Who the fuck are you to complain?"

In hindsight I should have taken a more conciliatory tone, of course, but it was just too much for me in the state I was in. I heard more than saw the chair break between his thighs as Aron got up. He wasn't all that tall, but he still filled the room. And my blood curdled as he spoke again, through his teeth this time, voice like grizzle. "You little piece of shit. You arrogant turd. You have no respect for anyone. Neither do I, but I have earned it, I have worked hard for it. I am superior. But you are just a snivelling pretender who hasn't earned his stripes. That doesn't cut it. Not in this game."

He nodded towards the gorilla who hauled me up by one

arm like a rag-doll and then held me still with his huge arms wrapped around me. Aron looked like a lunatic, his eyes wide open and a devilish mad grin. He pulled a baton with a small lanyard out of his pocket.

"This", he said as swivelled it around, playfully, drooling on one side of his mouth, "is 'the priest', the shaft is made of mahogany and the head is brass. it's meant for killing salmon, but I find it useful for a lot of things." He proceeded to grab my right foot, stretched my leg until I was horizontal between the two men, utterly helpless, and with the merest of action the head of the baton came down on my kneecap.

I barely heard the sickening sound of shattered bone and cartilage before the pain overtook me, and mercifully, it all went black.

Three Years Later

There were a lot of things about my own family I could no longer remember. The car accident was over ten years ago, and I was seventeen. But I did remember some of the words of wisdom my father would often recite: "Smart people learn from the mistakes of others. Stupid people don't even learn from their own mistakes." Those words have stuck with me like a valuable heirloom. To what degree I had heeded the saying was for others to judge, but at last I had retired from smuggling spirits, and I wasn't looking for any other dubious enterprises either.

I grabbed the bottle of Jack Daniels from the lounge-room table and went to the bathroom. Brad had persuaded me to come to a business school reunion, the five year anniversary party. It wasn't really my 'thing' any more, but it still hadn't taken too much persuasion. Before getting in the shower I took a swig of the bottle, felt the spirit kick-start my internal radiator, like a match to a gas-heater. Ever since that night in the bay my body had been suffering from permanent chills, and the best remedy I had found was alcohol.

I wrapped myself in the large, white, fluffy towel with the 'Carlton Hotel' logo, a souvenir I had 'acquired' on a recent business trip to London. As expected, I had been fired from my job. I got the letter the day I was admitted to hospital with a shattered kneecap. And that turned out to work in my favour; literally so, as it was seen as bad form to kick someone when they were down! I complained to the Employee Ombudsman, the lawyers got involved, my employer on the other side, with me in the middle. It could have turned out quite badly, but I had a rather combative labour rights lawyer on my side, who after two days in court managed to convince everyone, most importantly the judge, that I was the victim. I got my job back, received full compensation for time lost and my employer had to pay my legal fees. It was with considerable glee that I returned to work and promptly handed in my resignation.

I returned to the lounge-room with my bottle in hand. I grabbed one of four whisky tumblers on prominent display and filled it almost to the brim. Those four flutes were among my most treasured belongings, right up there with the furniture and ornaments I had kept from my parents home.

I was in hospital, just recovering from the operation on my knee, when three visitors arrived. It was Greg, the guy who had pulled me out of the water, and two other men I didn't recognise. They brought flowers and the four glasses that they had 'commandeered' from Jon Lauritzen's Fairlane, as Greg eloquently put it. The other two were the guys who had pulled Jon up and tried to resuscitate him. The police had told them I was suspected of having pushed Jon in, which they all felt was absurd, as I had put my own life at risk trying to rescue him!

When they had asked of my whereabouts, the police had informed them that I was in hospital. And that, of course, was also why the police was suspicious, that on the same day that Jon had drowned I ended up in hospital with a shattered kneecap, without a plausible explanation of how it had happened. I had told them I slipped on the bathroom floor, but couldn't explain why I was found fully clothed in bed when the ambulance arrived. And why had I told them earlier that I was living on Brad's boat because I was redecorating my apartment when that was clearly not the case? Lucky for me they did get hold of Brad in the Caribbean and he could confirm that he had indeed asked me to look after his boat, and that we were friends and he had no problems with my staying on the boat.

At one stage I did consider telling the police everything - the failed smuggling venture, Steve's murder, blackmailing Gunnar and about Aron's assault - but in the end I kept quiet.

The thought of prison and of confronting Aron in court did not appeal to me. So I stood my ground, shaky as it was, and rode the storm. Without a motive, no witnesses and no proof of any misdeeds, the police had no case, and the investigation eventually closed.

I picked up the remote control and turned on the stereo, found my favourite Calvin Harris CD and turned up the volume, enough for the glass table to vibrate slightly when the booming bass kicked in. The old lady in the apartment above mine was hard of hearing, and below me was a couple of young Swedish party-goers so I never had any complaints. I emptied the glass and walked into the bedroom, put on a brand new ensemble of pants, a nice shirt and cashmere wool blazer. Not bought for any particular occasion, but my finances were now OK, I could afford to indulge.

I had been fortunate, not just with the compensation and severance pay I received. Shortly afterwards, I ran into an old mate from business school, Roger Johnsen, who had just started a business importing furniture from China and was looking for a business partner. I still had the 450,000 left over from the smuggling debacle, so with a fictitious loan agreement, and a bit of creative accounting, I found myself a shareholder in 'Chinature Pty. Ltd.' In addition to our own retail outlet, we also won a few lucrative contracts outfitting hotels and offices. The future looked rosy.

After getting dressed and admiring my new outfit in the mirror, slicking back my hair, I sat back on the couch, refilled my glass, as well as a flask I duly slipped into the inside pocket of my blazer. I tried to keep to one bottle during the week. And one on the weekend, but it didn't always work out that way. My excuse was that I was always cold, which was true, but I was fully aware of my own self deception. I just did not have the motivation to change. To underline my weakness, I drank another large mouthful.

Brad was not due to pick me up for another 15 minutes. I opened my laptop and went to theworld.no website to see what was happening and to pass the time. War in Syria, war in Iraq, Israel firing missiles into Gaza and the Russians threatening to invade Ukraine. The hell with religion and the hell with Putin, the world was falling apart. Another reason to drink. I was just about to click onto the sports pages when another headline caught my attention: "The Factory Outlet Stores opening today". I opened the page: "'This is the end of the border trade', a large billboard formed like a STOP sign declares on the main freeway halfway between Oslo and the Swedish border. In record time, the Eastern District has a new major shopping centre set up to compete with the bargain shops across the border." I kept reading without learning anything new. It had been a while since I had last been reminded of the murder of Steve Hall.

I had, of course, followed everything written about his disappearance, and been quite shocked, but also relieved, when the police seemed to focus only on the death threats he had received. I had found the connection between Steve Hall, Gunnar Fergusen and the Factory Outlet Centre through a half hour of searching the internet. Maybe because I knew who the killer was. I had been considering an anonymous tip-off more than once, but the risk of exposing my own, rather dishonourable, involvement was too high. But still, the very thought of Steve Hall's fate remained distasteful to me, so I finished my drink. My mobile vibrated, a text from Brad: "2 mins". I stood up, turned off the stereo and the lights, grabbed my cane and walked outside.

Beatrice

A white limousine was waiting as I came out, and peering out from the large sun-roof was Brad and Kerry, bottle of Veuve Clicquot in hand, AC/DC playing at max volume on the stereo. "Party time!", Brad bellowed, his grin beaming at me. I had to laugh. Typical Brad. He was still living on the Island Gypsy, not because he couldn't afford an apartment, he was making good money in IT, but because he craved the freedom and loved the sea. And the contrasts. He was very much a non-conformist. I had told him everything when he returned from the Caribbean. He remained the only other person who knew the story.

I grabbed the bottle of champagne handed to me, had a swig before I got in the car. Just as well, the interior was a challenge to the senses - turquoise leather seats, plush red carpets and a pink light organ, a relic of the eighties. "Superbly tacky!" I shouted over the music, which made Brad's smile even broader. "Yeah!" shouted John and Arnie in unison from their leather seats, both already half drunk. The scene was set for a big night.

When we arrived at the business school campus about half an hour later I was both drunk and deaf. There were a few students about, grouped around books and laptops, looking serious. A few frowned as we walked unsteadily past them, others just laughed. A rather voluptuous woman from the office met us and asked us in a stern voice to calm down if we were to attend the party. We obliged. I was always good at pretending to be sober when drunk and put my arm around her waist, giving her my personal assurances that we'd all behave impeccably. She gave me a half smile, pressed her hip lightly against mine and said she'd hold me personally responsible if we didn't. I often had that effect on mature women. I liked to think that I aroused their maternal instinct.

The foyer of the main campus building had the look of a five-star hotel, including an internal glass lift. We arrived on the seventh floor where the party was held at the canteen. We were offered a welcome drink, a tepid fruit cocktail, and kept walking in, looking for faces we recognised. Lots of those, of course, most were worthy of just a nod, some of a high five, and a few a bear hug. Many asked me about my cane, smiling when I said "sports injury", an explanation readily accepted by most.

The cane and my limp could have made me look like a bit of a freak, not a common sight, but it was more the opposite. The cane was the perfect ice breaker with the ladies. "What happened to you? Does it hurt? Poor you." I was certain that some one-night stands I had were because the woman wanted to boast she'd slept with a cripple, kind of like a celebrity fuck. Not that I cared…

One of the girls from my class, the one that was a member of every committee that would have her, and now the chair of the reunion committee, held a short welcome speech. We were to be fed, and asked to queue up.

And that's when I saw her, just as we were amongst the last to join the line-up. Long, slender legs on high heels, disappearing up a tight, black leather mini skirt, a wide and elegant belt around an off-white silk blouse matching her blond hair, cropped fashionably short. I took a couple of deep breaths, one for her sheer beauty, the second for recognising who she was. The daughter of Gunnar Fergusen. She was quite simply stunning. Brad nudged me and laughed at something or someone he had seen, but I was distracted, couldn't help looking at her, trying not to be too obvious.

John and Arnie waved us over to their table, where they

had been joined by a group of average looking women, a couple of plus sized nymphs dragging the average further down. I turned around as I got seated and noticed her again, her name was Beatrice, wasn't it? She was now seated a few tables away, surrounded by a court of salivating would-be suitors, with more self-confidence than self awareness. Just as the woman next to me put her hand on my arm to say something, Beatrice turned and looked straight at me, with the most striking blue eyes I had ever seen. It felt like an earthquake, the epicentre in the core of my soul, the kind of quake you don't ever quite recover from. The woman next to me tugged at my arm, she had asked me a question. "Sports injury", I said, and she nodded at me with motherly sympathy.

Did Beatrice look at me on purpose, or was it just a sweeping glance? It felt like she was looking right at me, but then again I was drunk, so it was hard to be certain. Either way, Beatrice was the kind of woman I tried to steer clear of. I had made that mistake a couple of times before, smitten by beauty, albeit not quite in Beatrice's league. Both times it had felt like I had landed the big one, but the fear of losing the prey overshadowed the capture. So instead of enjoying the infatuation, let myself fall in love and wallow in their beauty, I became suspicious, jealous and moody. I became someone else, someone I didn't know, someone I detested, a loser. And it ended the way it had to, they soon lost interest, and I descended into my private black abyss of misery for a while.

I turned around to the girl next to me. She was more my type. Maybe a bit too much makeup, her dress too tight, but cute enough, if one didn't look too close. We started chatting about school and work. Brad already had his arm around one of the plus size girls. No surprises there, he was quite partial to a big, round ass as he liked to say.

A girlfriend of the girl I was talking to engaged her in conversation, so I turned around and looked towards Beatrice's table. The suitors were competing for her attention, gesticulating and laughing loudly without her appearing to engage much. She looked almost bored. And then she did it again, turned around and looked straight at me. Perplexed, I still managed a vague smile. She smiled back at me. There was no doubt this time. She was looking at me. Just me. A bit odd, considering we had attended the same school, different classes mind you, but for four years without ever exchanging a word. Could it be the cane? Was she just after a trophy fuck? Could be, and if so, it would be fine by me.

From experience I knew that women disliked indecisive men, especially the prettiest girls. Hesitate, and the opportunity is gone. Fresh suitors seemed to converge at her table so I decided to wait until dinner was over. I also didn't have the balls to walk to her table at that moment. So I continued to converse with the inferior alternative next to me, without too much enthusiasm.

At long last people had finished eating and were dutifully taking crockery and cutlery back to the kitchen. There was movement and I went with the flow. Found myself with a cup of coffee in hand. I looked around. Beatrice was nowhere to be seen, no longer at her table. Had she left? I panicked somewhat, surmising that the opportunity had been and gone; ignoring the little voice in the back of my head saying that Beatrice Fergusen was the last women in Oslo that I should get involved with tonight. Or anytime for that matter.

I wandered around the room, at the far end a bar had been set up, next to the DJ. She was standing in a corner, chatting to a couple of girlfriends. Better than before, but still not ideal, girlfriends can make things awkward. I abandoned the coffee and ordered a gin and tonic at the bar, focused on the DJ but with Beatrice in the corner of my eye. Four or five other blokes stood around, drink in hand, also glancing in her direction. Then one of the two girlfriends left. This was my best chance.

It was now or never.

I could be quite certain that Beatrice had heard all the pick-up lines ever conceived by drunken horny men, so I thought the direct approach would be best. I walked towards her, cane in my right hand, glass in the left, high on alcohol and anxious anticipation and said: "Let me just say that you are incredibly beautiful. And I am just about pissed enough to dare to tell you, and also pissed enough to handle a rejection, so I reckon it would be downright shameful not to have a go." She looked at me bemused, a slight smile forming, like a lifeline I could cling to.

On the one hand I'd handle her rejection, but there were a few blokes witnessing my advance, so the humiliation would no doubt be brutal. I was about to say my name when I picked up the refrain from The Clash song the DJ had just put on, so after a moment's hesitation, I intoned looking straight at her: "Should I stay or should I go."

She laughed out loud, grabbed the collar of my jacket and pulled me closer, saying "You should stay!" It was music to my ears. And as she let go, and my anxiety vanished, I saw how beautiful she really was: just a hint of eyeshadow, mascara and lip-gloss. That was all she needed. After exchanging names and after the girlfriend had sent me a filthy look before leaving, Beatrice put her hand on mine, put the glass to her mouth and one thigh between mine, and asked: "So, what's the deal with the cane, Marius?"

I pondered my reply for a second or two. I had three different stories I used: One for the caring, one for the gullible and one for the humorists. I was unsure which one to use. After all, she was the daughter of Gunnar Fergusen. On the other hand, what man would not take his chances with a woman like her? This is what life was about, get as high up the scale as possible. She was a tenner, and how many chances does a man get to max out on the top of the scale? Maybe a couple which I had already blown. So it was do or die, full steam ahead: "I'll tell you, but you probably won't believe me."

"Really? Do tell then", she said, mildly curious.

"OK then. A few years ago I did some parachuting. We were in Spain, a bunch of mates. A bit of free jumping, some formation jumps. Lots of fun." I paused for effect. She looked interested, but sceptical. "It was the last jump on the last day we were there. I was free falling, two hundred kilometres an hour, I hit a bird. My kneecap hit the bird on the head, or the other way around, if you like. Both shattered like an egg." She said nothing, her gorgeous eyes wide open, mouth half agape. A sight to behold, especially this close. "I said you wouldn't believe me", I exclaimed, feigning exasperation.

She looked bewildered, unsure if I was joking or not. "It sounds unbelievable. What are the odds of hitting a bird on the head with your kneecaps in mid air?"

"Not good. Maybe like winning Lotto and Powerball on the same day."

"And how come the skull of a small bird would shatter the kneecap of a grown man?"

"Thing is, whatever you hit at 200 km/h will do damage. Hit the brakes whilst driving at 80 km/h and a coke bottle in the back of your head from the backseat will kill you. But I agree. Almost too incredible to be true."

"Exactly. And someone once told me that if something is too incredible to be true, it usually is. Did you find the bird?"

"We did, actually. Otherwise we wouldn't have known what I had hit. The head was smashed to pieces. It was a brown Andalusian pigeon. Same colour as this", I said as I pulled the flask out of the pocket of my blazer.

She looked at me incredulously for a while. Then she started laughing loudly. A couple of people turned around. What a mouth. A perfect row of teeth. And there she was, mesmerised by one of my drunken tales. I was thrilled, but kept my cool. She grabbed the flask, removed the cork and drank without smelling it first. "Good ol' Jack", she said with her eyes closed and gave me the flask back. She placed a hand behind my neck. Pulled me closer and gave me a kiss; soft, lips wet and sweet tasting, the tip of the tongue, finishing with a quick, firm bite on my lower lip.

"I'll have to be careful with you, Marius. You are obviously full of it."

The mere fact that she said my name again was exciting. And when she lent her body into mine I sensed an odour, not perfume, not deodorant, not shampoo, but something primal. I answered: "Maybe. But if I had told you the truth, you would have started yawning. Boring like a Tuesday. Or like doing accounts."

She nodded, a quick laugh. We continued in the same vein, probing and prodding each other with questions and answers, ever closer, more personal. Oblivious to our surroundings, immersed in each other's words, hands touching, fingers entangling. I had a feeling of weightlessness, as if we were floating around in our very own bubble. She was in the middle of telling a funny story from a hens night, when one of her girlfriends burst through the bubble: "We can't be bothered anymore, Beatrice. We are going night clubbing. Are you coming?"

I froze. Would Beatrice leave me and go with them? Girls liked to stay together, afraid of leaving the fraternity of the night. I had experienced that phenomenon often enough. Maybe she'd ask me to come along? The moment of truth. Beatrice appeared undecided, she looked at her girlfriend, then back at me evasively. Her friend was impatient: "Beatrice, seriously, are you coming or what?" I felt the evening turning to shit. Bloody women! In pure frustration I stood up, took a theatrical step back and spread my hands out as if I was giving up. Beatrice reached out a hand and stroked my face, looking a bit sad, whispered "sorry", turned around and left.

I was stumped, disappointed and angry at the same time. Seriously! I'd never understand how women could be so dependent on each other. Then I thought of something I had read only a week ago, about a study revealing that 98% of the world's wealth was owned by men, women just 2%. No wonder, the bitches would never take a risk, so go figure! I picked up my cane and was about to walk out when someone tapped me on the shoulder.

As I turned around Beatrice shouted right into my ear: "Gotcha!" I looked straight into the most beautiful self-satisfied grin I had ever seen. "That's what you get for telling me porkies, Marius", she said with a laugh. "You should have seen yourself, like a little boy outside the lolly-store with a hole in his pocket." What a performance, I could only admire the way she had me fooled. Masterful. And at the same time I realised that the evening wasn't lost after all, she was mine, at least for tonight. I pulled her close, bit her earlobe in playful retaliation and said: "You well and truly had me fooled, so let's call it a draw. For now."

She excused herself to go to the toilet. I stood there waiting for her, protecting my turf, and then I spotted Brad lining up at the bar. I waved at him to come over. "I think I've got Beatrice Fergusen on the hook. You know the tall, blond, miss-fucking-unbelievable." He took a second or two to make the connection: "Sweet, Marius, sweet. A bit out of your league, but what can I say? I wouldn't say no, especially if she'd put on a few kilos here and there."

"You're a sicko, Brad, fuckin' sick. Maybe you are the one needing a few extra kilos so you could get it off with normal girls."

Brad considered that for a bit: "Interesting angle, I guess I'd have more to choose from then." He added: "She has a reputation as an absolute man-eater, and not one for offering seconds, either. But I guess you have that in common." He slapped me on the back and turned around to rejoin the bar queue. I held him back: "Her last name is Fergusen, she's the daughter of Gunnar Fergusen. You know the one."

Brad suddenly looked sober: "Oh my god, are you sure?" He paused: "Marius, that's not a great idea, you need to steer well clear of those people, you know that!"

Of course he was right. I looked at him: "I promise, just one fuck-and-go." He looked me straight in the eyes: "No, Marius, one fuck-and-run". Then he returned to the bar.

She was gone a long time, so long that I started thinking that she had left after all. At long last I saw her blond head gliding through the crowd, stopping a few times, but continuing towards me, and when she came close, she beamed a smile at me that could have knocked me over there and then. Good thing I was standing by the wall. She apologised for having been gone for so long, explained that she had to sort out the hens before they left. She rolled her eyes to underline how ridiculous she thought that was.

Her well coiffed hair curved perfectly around her long neck. I was mesmerised, drunk on her beauty as well as alcohol, and I blurted out without thinking: "How did you get to be so bloody beautiful?" I regretted saying it as soon as the words came out, what an inanely imbecile question. That was the drink talking. I had an apology ready, but she beat me to it: "My father sold his soul to the devil, so you are quite right." She said it like she meant it. I almost said that I knew, but thought better of it. She grabbed the flask from the pocket of my blazer and put it to my lips for a swig, then she drank what was left in the bottle. "Let's go", she said abruptly, her playful voice gone, replaced by a terse and commanding tone.

I could have bitten my tongue off. I didn't know if it was

my stupid question or the thought of her father she had reacted to. She grabbed my left hand and started pushing through the throng of revellers. Several tried to stop us, she ignored them all. Arnie saw me and hollered something, but I pretended not to notice. As we approached the glass lift, I noticed she wasn't walking straight in those high heels, she was tipsy.

She was still holding my hand, but said nothing. It was time to change the subject, so while waiting for the lift I pulled a well tested ace out of my sleeve: "This, Beatrice, is my party cane. It used to belong to the Emperor Haile Selassie of Ethiopia." I brandished the cane in front of her. "The shaft itself is made from the antler of a gazelle, and the handle is ivory, both from animals the emperor had shot himself. I won it in a bet with an African diplomat I met, he was certain that glass was a crystal, and I that glass is made from a heated, slow-running liquid. Needless to say, I was right, so the cane was mine."

She pulled the cane out of my hands and threw it over the railing where I could hear it break into pieces as it landed seven floors below.

"Fuck you, Marius, you are so full of shit", she said evenly, whilst at the same time grinding her ass into my groin. I was speechless. She was loopy. The doors to the lift opened and we got in, it was just the two of us in the lift overlooking the foyer below.

Halfway down Beatrice reached out an arm and hit the big red stop button, the lift came to a halt between the third and fourth floor. She pushed me up against one corner of the lift, and in one swift movement she unzipped my fly, pulled out my cock, adjusted her leather skirt and lifted one leg out to the side, and then instinct took over. It didn't take long before I was inside her, started breathing heavily, struggling to stay upright, when she engulfed me, her whole body shuddering as she came. It was primal, raw and unreal, surpassing any previous erotic encounters I'd had.

And we were on display. There were people watching from the foyer below and from the stairs above. As we exited the lift on the ground floor, we were greeted with applause and raunchy laughter from the small crowd of students, and a not so happy security guard. "You have to leave the building", he said gravely, although he was far too young to be taken seriously. But we were on our way out anyway so I replied: "You are right, we will", and with my hand on Beatrice's shoulder in the absence of my broken cane, we walked out. Outside, she stopped and kissed me. Passionately, and for a long time. Then she simply said: "Your place, or mine?"

Revenge

The next day I had 1.2 grams of Ibuprofen for breakfast, just before sunset. And it wasn't just my knee hurting.

We had been standing on the pavement outside the campus building for a bit, sparring over where to go. She wanted to go to my place; I wanted to go to hers. After a game of rock, paper, scissors which she lost by four to five we hailed a taxi. When we arrived at her place, I realised we were almost neighbours, just a few blocks apart. Her apartment was luxurious, minimalist and impersonal, a bit like a hotel suite. The most spectacular feature was the bedroom, mainly consisting of a huge, oval bed. The walls clad in a black and red textured fabric, same as the bedspread and a sea of decorative pillows, the colours of the Black Widow spider I thought as she pushed me down on the bed

When I woke up in the middle of the day, I had a peek under the duvet. Even while fast asleep she looked like a goddess. Her curves like the gentle undulation of sand dunes in the desert, accentuated by soft shadows. And the oasis in the middle, a well-trimmed dot of white hair. I was tempted to draw her close, but I was too spent for the inevitable consequence of another tryst, and continued to doze.

In the evening we ordered Pizza delivery and drank red wine. The triple dosage of Ibuprofen kept the throbbing in my knee at bay. For the first time we had a real conversation. She told me she ran her own consultancy in international marketing analysis. Travelled a fair bit, mainly overseas, London her most frequent destination. I thought to myself that I would like to be a fly on the wall when she met her clients for the first time. I stayed another night as a matter of course, no questions asked. We made love again. Not as wild and intense, but for longer. Still fantastic. When she fell asleep snuggled up next to me, her head on my chest, I thought that this might just be the pinnacle, that I would look back on this moment as the best life had to offer.

I left around midday on Sunday. We exchanged mobile numbers. Agreed to meet again for dinner later in the week. The farewell kiss lingered long. Something had happened, for both of us. In the taxi home I felt strongly drawn back to her.

I wasn't quite sure if this was the beginning of a 'committed relationship'. It was too early for that. And I was also preoccupied with another project which had been taking up most of my spare time during the last few months, and was soon to be put into action. After that fateful day three years ago, my life had changed irrevocably. And not entirely for the better. If it had just been a matter of single surgery, eight weeks of recovery and reconditioning, then that would have been OK. I could have written it off as a lesson learnt. But it wasn't like that.

My kneecap had been splintered in three and had to be kept together with pins and wires. After a while it became clear that the pieces were not knitting together properly, the wounds became infected, and a new operation was required, where they also removed the shrapnel. The infection healed, but the pain remained, so I started consuming Ibuprofen like it was candy. And even if I did a lot of strengthening exercises, the knee still felt like it could pop at any time. The doctors were considering a complete knee replacement in titanium and resin. My football career, to the extent that it could have been called a career, was over. And I was still in my mid twenties. The same went for most other physical activities. Quite simply a personal catastrophe.

But what I could also not accept, what I found unforgivable, was the absolute futility of it. Aron had got his money back, with twice the interest, before the due date, but he still chose to hurt me. And that I could not accept as just a lesson learnt, because it was so unnecessary. Hence the thought of revenge kept coming, first during the day, and then keeping me awake on many a night. The thoughts festered, turning into profound hatred. Eventually, about three months ago, Aron became a marked man.

The first decision I had to make was how far I'd go to satisfy my thirst for revenge. In a recurring dream, where Aron transformed into a walrus, I harpooned him, his remnants running like rivers of blood, bile and blubber. I always woke up with a start, but with a good feeling. The question was, did I have the guts to point a gun at Aron and pull the trigger? Maybe, maybe not. I didn't think I'd know the answer until I had tried. But after a while it kind of sorted itself out. I wanted him to suffer at least as much as I had, preferably more. And suffering, in my godless philosophy of life, belonged to the living, not the dead, an important insight under the circumstances.

The problem of letting him live, was the risk of retaliation. I considered planting child pornography on his computer and then tipping off the police, having heard how paedophiles were treated in prison. Unfortunately, my IT knowledge was not adequate for me to do that without being caught in the act.

I conferred with Brad who was of the opinion that it would be hard to hide one's tracks, at least from the experts. Other such ideas were dismissed on similar grounds. To have a chance, I had to find a weakness I could use. A Google search only revealed some articles related to Torpedo Pizza, many more related to his weightlifting prowess, where nowadays he appeared to be more of a mentor to younger competitors. Poor kids, I thought. But I found one thing which piqued my interest: he lived in the same street as he worked. He lived in no. 7, but worked at no. 10. A practical arrangement for sure, short commute, but still a bit peculiar.

One night when I was in the neighbourhood, I drove through the short cross street he lived in. Apart from the cast iron gate at the back of Torpedo Pizza, and the restaurant itself, the street consisted of old low-rise apartment blocks, a small park with a playground and a couple of street benches. No. 7 was opposite the park, about 50 metre away and diagonally across from his home at no. 10. It struck me as the perfect place for a set-up. It was literally his own backyard. He'd feel safe here. Aron was clever, street-wise, almost impossible to outsmart. But here was an opportunity, the question was how? I parked nearby, walked down to the little park. In the corner of the park was a small shed. An idea started forming in my head.

Ronald, my passionate sports-fishing buddy, had bought himself a mini-camera to capture his marine life accomplishments. It looked like a Maglite torch, and could record up to three hours of continuous video. As it was near the end of the fishing season, he let me borrow it. A couple of days later I went back to the shed in the evening and mounted the camera just under the eaves, out of sight from any casual passers-by. It pointed straight at the entrance to the apartment block that Aron lived in. I timed it to start at 6am and to record at wide-angle.

The next evening I retrieved the camera and connected it to my laptop as soon as I got home. Aron was the first person to appear, at 6:13, traversing the street towards the pizza place. He must have been in a good mood that morning, because halfway there he did a little skip, like a dance step. Good for you, I mused. I kept watching the footage, but didn't see Aron again. Every available evening for the next two weeks I did the same, mounting the camera in the same place. And every time I saw the same, between 6:09 and 6:14, he came out, walked the same way and did the same dance step. What was he doing? Maybe it wasn't so much a dance step, more like a kick, planting his left foot firmly down and kicking an imaginary ball with his right. One night I walked down the street to look closer, and where I thought he performed his little routine, there was a manhole cover.

A couple of nights later I returned with the camera and a stepladder. On the pavement across from the manhole there were a few Mountain Ash trees, one of them had a split trunk and I managed to mount the camera in the groove where they separated. Getting up and down with the help of the stepladder was a painful reminder of why I was doing this. I could only hope that nobody would notice the little camera before I could retrieve it.

Nobody did, and the footage was revealing. As he walked, Aron planted his left foot right in the middle of the manhole cover and then kicked straight at a football that wasn't there. That was it. And he did it every day, even on Sundays. I couldn't know, but I envisaged that he was born on this street, that he still lived in his childhood home. Why else would a seemingly successful businessman live in an old and tired apartment block in this part of town? Nostalgia, he had his roots there. Maybe he had walked the same way to get to school and done the same every morning, imagining he was blasting the winning goal in a football game. A great feeling, and a good start to the day. So he had just continued to do it.

The next evening I was back, photographing and measuring the manhole cover. It had a three-pointed star with the number 40 in the middle, surrounded by the customary pattern of small protrusions. It was 65 centimetres in diameter and very heavy as you'd expect. For some reason it gave me associations of the Nazi swastika. I had brought a crowbar and lifted the cover so I could see what was in the hole. It was about three metre deep, a pipeline with a turning valve at the bottom. I put the cover back as I had found it, wiping off any marks I had made. I was thinking that yes, this could work. I just had to drink on it.

Which I did. Several times. And when drunk the plan seemed both ingenious and foolproof. When sober I considered the outcome was uncertain, but that it definitely could work. As I had no alternative plan, I resolved to give it a go.

It took several days to find the right piece to use, and I ended up with an old wooden kitchen bench. I bought a vice, a circle-saw, a wood-planer, sandpaper of various grit, and an assortment of chisels. Paid cash. I sawed, sanded and drew patterns, before carefully starting to chisel, aware that any false cuts would ruin my work. I was surprised at how much I enjoyed it. Started to get the knack, too, maybe a new hobby for a half cripple in the future? When finished I had a round wooden plate, 65 centimetre in diameter, 3.5 centimetres thick at the edges, but thinner in the middle and with three air holes. Not far from where I lived I found a similar manhole and used the crowbar to lift it and moved it aside. I put my handy-work over the hole and it didn't quite fit. Maybe it wasn't quite round. Had to sand it down a few millimetres around the edges. A few hours later I returned, and this time it fit like a glove.

Perfect. But not the right colour. I started experimenting with the many off-cuts, trying different variations of wood coatings, and found just the right shade, a mixture of sandy grey and dark farmhouse red. But it still didn't look like metal. A trip to the local hobbyist store and I found a spray paint that resembled the coppery iron of the original. It was a piece of art to be proud of, I'd happily hang it on my wall, maybe even enter an art exhibition. I had recently read that a urinal had been declared the most important work of art of the twentieth century. Hard to say whether it was the century or the artists that was the problem. Not that this ruined my sleep. I took my cover-art back to the manhole and compared it again. Very similar, except for the dirt. I found an old pizza box and with some effort I tipped the manhole cover over it to capture the dirt, and then drizzled it onto my piece. It looked natural. I just couldn't see how this wouldn't work.

Finally, I hid all other evidence of my creation. I cleaned all the tools and placed them in a heavy duty garbage bag which I dropped off under a large rock in the woods on the outskirts of town. Just in case something went wrong and I had to start again. I disposed of all the paint, the sand paper and the spray-cans. I vacuumed my apartment thoroughly and got rid of the vacuum bags. I finished with a full dust and clean. Deleted anything I had downloaded to help with my creation, including my recent search history. I wasn't all that concerned that I would be a suspect. I could be quite certain that Aron, after decades of criminal activity, had a long list of enemies well before my name. But should he show up, I wanted to be certain there would be nothing to connect me to what was about to happen. I felt ready.

Then Beatrice came on the scene. Not that it mattered, but I put my plan on hold. The tension between falling in love with Beatrice and the hatred for Aron was intense. It made me anxious and indecisive, not a good starting point.

I invited Beatrice for dinner as agreed. She said she liked Asian, so I booked a table at a chic pan-Asian restaurant with a sushi bar. The din of the restaurant lowered perceptibly as she arrived fashionably late, sashaying towards my table where I was nurturing a whisky. Again, I was breathless, I had butterflies in my tummy and my head was swimming as I stood up for a generous welcoming kiss. What little clothing she was wearing seemed like it was sprayed on. I heard an audible gasp from the table next to ours.

Food and drink was ordered and served, everything top-shelf, although it all seemed like unnecessary props. We talked, kissed and touched, above and below the table, and I half expected the maitre d' would come over and ask us to leave. We talked about school, the Oslo night-life and the English Premier League, a subject she surprisingly knew as much about as I did. Family and work were not mentioned. When I asked why she had thrown my cane over the railing, she laughed and called me an incurable liar. She contended that anyone who told such outrageous lies deserved suitable recriminations. "So what if it's true?", I asked. "Well, Marius", she said and reached across the table, "then I am in big trouble. Maybe I won't even get a fuck tonight. But I don't believe that either."

I was hooked. Her raw charm and stunning looks were overwhelming me. I kept up as best as I could, but felt that at any time she would swallow me whole and spit me out in the gutter. But she didn't. She wanted me. And I relented, willingly, even if the story of the cane was true enough.

We spent the weekend at my place, most of it in bed. The more we made love, the stronger the desire, the wilder the sex, at times almost lethally so. But we couldn't stop. I was almost relieved when she told me she was going to London for the week. And when the all-consuming Beatrice was no longer there, my focus returned to Aron. I had prepared and planned everything. What would happen when Beatrice returned next Sunday and beyond, I could not know. All my pain, the complications, the ingrained hatred, it was all embedded in the round piece of wood. By now I had an almost religious belief that this would set me free. I decided on doing it Thursday, the day of Thor - the Warrior God.

~ ~ ~

I was there about an hour early. The wooden cover and the crowbar in a box that I was pushing in front of me on a hand trolley. I was dressed with a hood, a cap and gloves, all black, numb with extra doses of Ibuprofen to minimise the limping. If anybody saw me, I would be hard to identify or describe. It was quiet, nobody around. I was nervous. This was serious.

I sat down in the little park and waited. A taxi arrived and stopped outside no. 5, a light went off on the third floor, a woman came out and got into the cab. She looked like she was wearing a uniform, maybe a stewardess. It was too dark to see if the taxi drove over the manhole, but it was possible as it was right in the middle of the road. For that reason I didn't want to replace the cover too far in advance.

I waited until 5:45. Rolled the box to the manhole. Listening. Now or never. I took the crowbar and lifted the cover. Then slowly, as quietly as I could, dragging it away from the hole. Then I put down the wooden replica, it fitted snugly, and I carefully aligned the patterns in the same direction as the original. Finally, I put the real cover on the trolley and rolled it down to outside the Torpedo Pizza entrance. There you go. Door to door service.

I should of course have gone straight to the car and driven away, there was nothing more I could do, but I just had to witness it. I positioned myself on the other side of the park, leaning against the corner of a house, looked at my mobile like everybody does when waiting these days. Then I heard something unexpected - mechanical, hydraulics - it was the garbage truck. I froze. What if it ran over the manhole with one wheel? What if one of the garbos stepped on it?

There was nothing I could do about it, would just have to let it happen. It was 6:03 when the truck stopped right outside Aron's house, right on top of the manhole. One of the garbos entered the garbage shed, another was dragging two bins behind him. Aron could be there any second. I was no longer leaning casually against the house, I was standing erect and looking intensely at the garbage truck, like an expectant kid.

Sound of a Murder

The bins were lifted up, flipped over and emptied with a mechanical shake. The two garbos continued to the next house and the truck moved on.

That was close. It was a cold morning, but I was sweating. The danger had passed. I looked around, a man was walking on the other side of the street I was on. I resumed my earlier position, staring at the gate to Aron's block. Time stood still. It was 6:12. The gate swung open and a very large man came out. There was no doubt. It was him. I counted down the seconds. When I reached zero, he had taken the last step. His left foot was on its way down.

I was quite certain that I heard a crack before I heard the scream. Which reverberated between the walls of the buildings making the whole scene seem surreal, as in the famous Edvard Munch painting. And then it stopped. All I could see was his torso above the manhole, lifeless, I thought he might have fainted. Then I heard weak groans. He started swaying back and forth, tried to push himself up with his massive arms, but it looked like he was stuck. The groaning continued, it sounded like he was in serious pain. "Serves you right, you scoundrel", I whispered to myself. At the same time I was starting to get anxious. It was time to go. I was just about to turn around when Aron just disappeared down the hole. Literally off the face of the earth.

The trip home was an emotional roller coaster, from the ecstasy of Aron's pain and disappearance, to the fear of having been seen, even a misplaced moment of sympathy. I sat in my kitchen with a glass of whisky and tried to assess what had happened. It had all gone to plan. The wooden cover had cracked, he had hurt himself falling, most likely broken something. For a man weighing 200 kilos that was non-trivial. It was just what I wanted, to inflict long-term pain. The disappearance down the well was merely a bonus.

During the day the story appeared on the net. The World newspaper site had pictures of a fire truck and the heading: "Dangerous manhole cover removed!" I kept reading: "Earlier today, a local businessman fell down into a sanitation well outside his own home. According to the police, the manhole cover had been replaced by a wooden replica which broke when the man stepped on it. The ambulance and the fire brigade had great difficulty getting the man up due to his condition and considerable girth, and in the end they had to get a tow truck to lift him out. The police on the scene announced: 'This is a serious matter, it was either a very bad practical joke or a deliberate act of malice, and we are investigating accordingly.'" By the evening, the story was everywhere online. Several used the 'bad joke' angle, but one pointed out that the victim was well known in criminal circles, and that it could well have been an act of revenge. I had to smile.

~ ~ ~

The next morning the story had been elevated to the front pages. A senior surgeon at the Oslo Hospital announced that the victim had a broken ankle, had a badly fractured hip, as well as having suffered a stroke. He was in a critical condition. That unsettled me. What if he died? Was that OK? I had an internal debate about it and concluded that it was. He was a scoundrel and a scumbag, and he always would be. A dead scoundrel is a good scoundrel, I concluded, and could no longer hurt me.

Beatrice rang Saturday afternoon and said she'd get on a plane and get home that same evening, and could I pick her up at the airport. Of course, I could. And I have to admit that standing in the arrivals hall watching Beatrice come towards me with her irresistible smile and throw herself at me was good for my soul. The envy, that most Norwegian of virtues, was so blatantly evident amongst the men in the vicinity that I was almost embarrassed. People looked at us as if we were celebrities. Can't deny I was enjoying it.

The weeks went by. Neither of us said it out aloud, we were lovers, in a relationship. In between I worked hard, got stuff done, and then we had a couple of days together. And nights. It was the same for her. She'd be away for a few days, busy some nights, and then she had all the time in the world. It worked. And best of all, I managed the pressure, I stood firm. One day there was a story in the paper about the man who had fallen down the manhole, the owner of Torpedo Pizza, he was recovering, no longer in a critical condition, but would have to endure a long period of rehabilitation. The police had nothing to go on. It all suited me just fine. I couldn't remember being happier.

Then one day, about a month after the reunion party, Beatrice asked me if "please, please, please" would I join her at her parents mutual 50th birthday party.

Birthday Party

The question hit me like a thunder-bolt. Neither of us had talked about our families, nor asked any questions. Consciously or subconsciously, family had been a non-topic. As a result, I had also not run the risk of blurting out Gunnar's name. Brad had repeatedly cautioned me against my liaison with Beatrice, but his warnings had fallen on deaf ears. I was hopelessly in love.

When the question came, I immediately tried to wriggle out of going: "Isn't it a bit early to get the family involved?" "I am not good with formal gatherings", and "I think I might be in China on business that week", but nothing worked. At first she was disappointed, then angry, and then the tears came. Real tears. And who can resist the tears of their lover? What was the likelihood of Gunnar recognising me? During our short encounter when I got the money I had a hood on, and he had only very briefly looked up at me from the car seat. I had said a few words, but as I recalled, my voice had been deep and gravelly, not like my voice at all.

That was it. It was more than unlikely that he would now recognise me three years later, in an entirely different context, so in the end I relented: "Beatrice, if this is so important for you, I will make every effort to be able to attend." Her smile returned. I wiped away a tear from her chin. I was fucked.

The next time we met she explained herself a bit more. Growing up, Beatrice had been the apple of her father's eye, cute, sweet natured and placid, treated like a princess. Gunnar had loved bringing her to work, showing her off, even taking her on business trips abroad. The company grew, and Gunnar probably envisioned that as an only child she would one day take over the business. That all changed when she became a teenager. Beatrice had become a bit of a rebel, sneaking out at night, hanging out with much older adolescents, partying, drinking and the typical mischief, enough to have both the police and the child protection authorities visiting their home. When she was 15, her father threw her out of the house for the first time. After that, she lived with her mother, Vivian, in an apartment, and at times they'd both be allowed back in the family home. As soon as she finished High School, Beatrice had moved to downtown Oslo by herself.

Mother and daughter were close. They had always supported each other, her mother acting as the peace keeper between father and daughter. Vivian had pleaded with her to come to the party, she didn't think she could handle it without her. And Beatrice felt the same way, she needed someone by her side on the night. There were too many impertinent idiots in her parents circle of friends who would use the occasion to poke and prod into old stories and fresh rumours. There were plenty of those. But with me at her side, a stranger, they wouldn't be able to. I could see her point, but asked the obvious question: "If your dad is such an ass-hole, why doesn't your mother just leave him?" Beatrice looked at me with sad eyes: "I have often wondered about that, too. And I honestly don't know. There is the financial side of things. Dad owns the company and the farm, a large part of which was sold for a small fortune a few years ago. And then there is the fact that once upon a time mum was a very attractive woman. Now she's a borderline alcoholic, a fifty-year-old who looks sixty. Where would she go? What would she do? Dad rules the roost with an iron fist. He'll never let her go."

A month later we were driving to the party. It was a beautiful autumn day, the sun was shining and it was almost hot. On the way there we passed the spot where my mum and dad and my sister had been killed, but I didn't say anything. Beatrice was unusually quiet, but I supposed she had her own demons to struggle with on the day. I was rather nervous about meeting Gunnar, even though I was certain that he wouldn't recognise me. If he did, I would vehemently deny everything, and then go straight to the police.

The party was to be held at the Fergusen family farm where Beatrice had spent her early childhood. Her mother had offered us a guest room in the main house, but fortunately, Beatrice had declined. We had booked a room in a small hotel not far from there.

Our relationship had settled down a bit, it was no longer all about the sex. She worked sporadically, would be away for a few days, during which I would work long hours. When we spent time together, we'd go to a cafe and talk, enjoy people watching, read. We'd go to the movies and attend concerts, all the normal things that lovers do. One Saturday afternoon we were walking around one of the shopping arcades in Oslo when we stopped in front of a gallery. There was a black-and-white photo, maybe one by two metre, of a naked woman on a deserted beach. Even though it was from behind, I recognised who it was. We entered the gallery and were greeted by Morten, the owner and the photographer who embraced Beatrice warmly and pleaded for the chance of another shoot with her.

I surveyed the photograph further. I didn't claim to know much about art in general or photography in particular, but this one I could understand: lines and curves, light and shade, land and water, black and white. It was simple and at the same time perfectly complete, one could almost ignore the obvious eroticism of it. If I didn't have access to the original, I would have bought it on the spot, even at the 15,000 asking price. But above all I was proud, pleased as punch that it was me she wanted, that it was me who would join her under the duvet at night. Life was wonderfully unpredictable. A couple of days later she gave me a blow-job whilst I was driving on the ring-road during rush hour.

On our way to the party we drove past huge posters advertising the Factory Outlet Stores. Beatrice told me that it had been built on land owned by her father and that he and his mates had made millions on the development. "Last year dad bought a huge bloody boat, a Princess worth ten million", she concluded contemptuously. I kept my thoughts to myself.

The receptionist at our hotel was an old acquaintance of Beatrice's and we were upgraded to the bridal suite. Beatrice asked for champagne to be sent to the room, so we could test it out appropriately. Afterwards she fell asleep, and I lay awake for a while just looking at her. Occasionally I had the feeling that I would lose her, and that she was starting to get bored with me. Didn't think I'd tackle that very well.

I woke her up at 4:30. The party started at 6. I had showered and was sitting naked in bed drinking champagne while she showered and got ready. Through a mirror on the wall I could see her applying makeup. She did her hair with a curling iron in a couple of minutes. Then, like the most natural thing in the world, she put a finger up her snatch and then behind each ear. I must have made a sound, because she peered at me through the bathroom door, obviously aware of what I had just seen: "What about it Marius, don't look like you have just dropped down from the moon. It's one of the oldest tricks in the book. The best perfume known, full of pheromones, irresistible to any man. Never let me down, anyway", she laughed and walked naked towards me. From time to time I had the feeling she was exactly like Brad had said: "Out of your league."

Neither of us talked during the cab ride. We held hands, two sweaty palms pressed together. Beatrice was wearing a turquoise dress with a high split and deep cleavage, which would undoubtedly be a talking point during the evening. But it was otherwise unusual to see her like this - quiet and vulnerable. She had not visited the farm for several years. The taxi drove past the Factory Outlet Stores and continued around the back of the centre. The parking lot was half full, not bad for a Saturday afternoon in early October. Strange to think that it had been made possible by a murder, and that I could most likely have stopped the whole project with a five second call to the police tip-off line. But even more unbelievable was that I was about to meet the murderer himself, possibly even my future father-in-law.

Didn't know if I should laugh or cry. I looked at Beatrice. She had a furrowed brow and lines on her face that I hadn't seen before. I kissed her cheek. She smiled and squeezed my hand a bit harder. We went over a crest and then the farm came into view. A tall, old birch adorned the front of the house, splendidly dressed for a party in the magnificent colours of autumn. On each side of the main house was a barn and a storehouse of the traditional kind, the first floor sitting on elevated stumps. There were fairy lights hanging everywhere, more reminiscent of Christmas than of a birthday party. Well-dressed guests stood around in groups, sipping pink coloured drinks with a slice of orange and the obligatory umbrella.

I paid the driver and stepped out of the car with Beatrice behind me. We stood there for a few seconds, as if on the red carpet waiting for the flashes from the cameras. Many turned around and looked, a few waved discreetly, with some putting their heads together talking in hushed voices.

A few broke away from their groups and came towards us. A girl who had already had a few too many pink drinks threw herself at Beatrice shouting "Beatrice darling!" I was soon introduced to acquaintances, neighbours and relatives as I looked anxiously for the only face I would know. Then I spotted Vivian, unmistakably her daughter's mother, the same blond hair, the same big smile. She came towards us, arms outstretched, and people stood aside, gave her the space. It was still evident that she had been a beautiful woman once, but the ravages of time had not been kind to her. Her face puffy, the wrinkles too deep, carrying too many kilos. Only the glint in her eyes when hugging her daughter seemed genuine. "This is my boyfriend, Marius", Beatrice said and pulled me forward. It was the first time she had called me her boyfriend.

I was momentarily taken aback, a bit flustered when saying: "Pleasure to meet you. Thanks for having me, and happy birthday!" She smiled and said thank you. I was just about to comment on how the farm looked lovely, and on how well decorated it was for the party, when Gunnar emerged from the barn. The words stuck in my craw. He was staring at me. Did he recognise me, a sudden and unpleasant recollection from a dark past? Had I made the most unforgivable miscalculation? I smiled at something Beatrice had said to her mum, keeping tabs on Gunnar out of the corner of my eye. He stood still, hesitating, before walking determinedly towards us: "What a pleasure to see you both. Welcome!" He gave Beatrice a perfunctory quick hug and then he reached out a hand. I shook his hand and introduced myself. His handshake was firm, his gaze wary and the smile forced, as if he smiled with his teeth only. Apart from that, there was no reaction that indicated he knew who I was. Again I was about to comment on the beautiful surroundings and the decorations when he looked straight past me, slapped me on the shoulder, said we should have a chat later, and continued to greet another group of guests.

Beatrice leaned in close and whispered: "I think he likes you. Otherwise he would have punched your lights out." I snickered and pinched her arm. "Come", I said, "let's drink all his alcohol." She nodded, took her mum by one arm and me by the other, and together we walked towards the table with the over-sized pink bowl.

An hour later we were seated at a long table with 120

guests inside the barn. It was a lavish spread, as was the alcohol content in the pink drink, it was potent. Gunnar was at one end of the table, Vivian the other, and Beatrice and I had been placed in the middle. Go figure. And the food was great, gravlax, roasted wild boar, and a traditional dessert of cinnamon infused apple crumble layered with rich cream, a traditional Norwegian favourite. All accompanied by plenty of quality wine. The party would have cost hundreds of thousands.

Judging by the speeches, Gunnar was one standout guy, generous to a fault, helpful and loyal to his friends. Vivian likewise. At every lie Beatrice pinched my thigh under the table, so much so that I had to ask her to stop. Beatrice was not mentioned in any of the speeches, as if she didn't exist. It was obvious that the truth was more evident by what wasn't said. That was OK by me. I was already drunk and excited at the thought of the bridal suite waiting for us.

After dinner coffee was served with a selection of cognac, liqueurs and ports. I was at a table with Beatrice and Vivian and five or six others, including one guy named Joe. There was a Joe there on the night Steve Hall had been murdered. I recalled the class photograph with Vivian and Gunnar, Joe was the short, blond boy at the left in the front row. While Beatrice and her mother circulated, I started talking with him. Cannot remember what we talked about, but I found him quite pleasant and polite. He was engaging and a good listener, a rarity amongst drunk, Norwegian males. I thought of the fact that he too had been there that night, drawn into Gunnar's devilish deeds. It seemed so inappropriate to get a man like him involved. Sensitive souls should be spared. The ones involved should be those who could take the punishment. Involuntarily, I stroked the scar on my knee with my index finger.

The ladies were using the toilet in the main house, the men had to go behind the barn for a piss. As I stood there for maybe the third time, I felt a hand on my shoulder. I turned around and looked straight into Gunnar's face. "So this is the bloke who is fucking my daughter." He pretended to be stern, but he didn't seem to say it to scare me. It sounded more like a joke. He chuckled after he had said it.

"Maybe it's the other way around", I blurted out. I regretted it straight away, and even though I knew it was true enough, I realised that it was a bit much; on his birthday, about his daughter, at his farm. On the other hand he had set the tone. His reaction was immediate. He punched me in the back with an outstretched arm, I lost my balance and fell forward, face first in my own piss. "Who the hell do you think you are?" he yelled out standing over me. "Coming here being a fucking smart-ass", he yelled again and kicked me in the side.

A couple of men came around the barn, I tried to get up, but Gunnar put his foot on my back and pressed down. One of the men ran up to Gunnar and pulled his right arm. "Gunnar, what's up?"

"What's up? I'll tell you what's up! This little shithead is telling me that, that, that Beatrice…"

"Calm down, Gunnar. It's just drunken talk. Come here", he said as he tried to pull Gunnar away. The other man had also arrived and was holding his left arm.

"Even if you are right, Gunnar, you can't take it out on a cripple. That's not right, mate." Gunnar tried to kick me again, but missed. "Fuck it, Gunnar, give it a miss. He's down on the ground. Come on, let's have a drink." The two men took him by the arms and guided him back around the corner of the barn.

I retrieved my cane and tried to get up. The side of my torso was tender, but nothing had been broken. I stumbled back on my feet. As I wiped dirt and grass off my pants, another man came towards me. At first I thought he was going to continue where Gunnar had left it, but he didn't. "You have to excuse Gunnar", he said, "he can be difficult, especially when he's had a few. What happened?"

"A stupid misunderstanding, that was all", I answered.

"Ah well, welcome to the countryside, where all parties end in a brawl. Unfortunately today it was your turn." He helped wipe the dirt off my jacket before continuing: "But it's best if you and Beatrice get out of here. Somebody has already called a taxi."

"Thanks, that sounds like a good idea. I am sorry about the fuss", I said, and I meant it.

"Listen", he said as if to reassure me, "you are not the first to have managed to upset Gunnar when he's drunk. I have too, and you won't be the last. Just look after Beatrice, and it will all be OK." He pointed towards the main entrance. "There is the taxi. I'll go with you, Beatrice will meet us there."

When we got into the backseat of the cab, I was about to tell her what happened, but as soon as I opened my mouth hers was already there, and she didn't let go until we rolled up outside the hotel. "The local cab-drivers love to gossip", she slurred as we staggered towards the door.

After some small talk with the receptionist and some groping in the hallway, we got into our room and I told her what happened behind the barn. "Did you really say that", she gasped and hit me in the chest.

"Yes, sorry Beatrice. I didn't mean to. It just happened. And I didn't mean it like that, either."

She started laughing. "Oh yes, Marius, you did. You think I am a nymphomaniac. And the first thing you say to dad, except for your name, is just that. Un-fucking-believable." She tilted her head back and laughed uproariously. "Don't you get it? He's the only one who could talk about me like that. If others do it, he loses it completely. He still hasn't decided if I am Madonna or a whore. The man is crazy."

I felt like a dickhead, but couldn't help laughing. "And I was about to ask Gunnar for your hand in marriage. Do you reckon I should go back and ask him?"

Beatrice couldn't help herself. "You do that, Marius, you do that. And if you do, I'll say yes. And then we get married."

"OK, let me get this straight, if I go back and ask Gunnar, then you'll marry me?" I knew this was just a game, of course, but a small part of me was considering it - somebody would marry her one day, might as well be me!

"Then I'll marry you, Marius … You'll have to go now, before he goes to bed." She chortled, sent me a provocative glance.

What else could I do but play along? So I grabbed my jacket and my cane and walked towards the door. I was hoping she'd stop me, but she didn't, so I went out into the hallway and closed the door behind me. There I stopped, heart in my throat, listening. I was pretty sure she was doing the same on the other side of the door, but not quite. After a couple of minutes I saw the door-handle move. I took a few steps back, pretending I came walking back from the reception, when she opened the door and peered out.

"Hi", I said, "what a coincidence. I met your father outside. He said to say hello. He had come to apologise. I told him that it was OK provided he let me marry his daughter, which he thought was a terrific idea. So when would it suit you, Beatrice? How about a spring wedding? Maybe we can have the ceremony at the farm, under the big birch?"

She pulled me back inside and pushed me down on the bed, before lifting her dress and straddled me, grabbed my wrists and held me down, her sumptuous tits overflowing the top of her dress. "You little man, you didn't dare. Just like all other men, you've got no balls." She grabbed the evidence to the contrary as if to confirm. "That's Right. Nothing." She said, looking content.

I had to laugh. How many women had made me laugh like

that? None. Not even close. I tried to get my hands free, but she put all her weight on top of me. Then she said: "I can't marry a sissy, Marius. I'm sure you'll understand that. What have you done to deserve to be my prince, anyway? Except for insulting my dad?" I pressed my hips against hers, I knew what she wanted. "Yes, yes, Marius, and except that."

So that's how she wanted to play it. She wanted to test me, see if I was man enough for her, or more to the point, if I was crazy enough for her. That felt OK by me. There and then I felt invincible as if nothing could hurt me. And shit-faced. Straddling me was the woman of my dreams challenging me. No way I would yield, give her an even bigger advantage, so I said: "Well, Beatrice, since you ask, I have a history of smuggling spirits into Norway, if that's the kind of thing you had in mind?"

"So what Marius, you've been to Majorca and come back with a couple of bottles more than the allowed quota through customs?" She loved mocking me, but maybe this time I could get back at her.

"Nope, more like 20,000 bottles too many."

"Liar, liar, pants on fire", she laughed.

"Fifty kroner a bottle, cost me a million, made me three million. On a semi-trailer from Poland", I said as I thrust my hips up again. She loosened the grip around my wrists, sat up, looked at me sharply.

I returned her gaze and said: "Financed my four years of Business School. Lock, stock and barrel." She nodded pensively. Beatrice knew about my extravagant lifestyle as a student.

"Not bad, Marius, not bad. Maybe you'll do after all." She was still straddling me, moved back and forth, just to reinforce her dominance. But I had obviously jolted her, a rare chance that I could not pass up, so I said: "And what about you, Beatrice, have you got anything illicit on your CV, or is it just talk?"

She winced, but I could tell that she liked the question: "I can at least match that, Marius. Strangely enough we have been in a similar trade, you and I, but I have kept to a commodity of more lasting value. Gold."

"Yeah right, gold, sure", I said, trying to read her. But she kept a straight face, looked down at me as if I was a little kid. "You are serious", I continued, "you have smuggled gold? I don't get that, how can you make money on gold? Isn't the gold price the same world-wide, dollars per ounce?"

Again the slightly condescending smile, before she answered. "No, Marius, that's not quite the case. Norway is one of the few countries charging sales tax on gold bars, so as soon as it crosses the border, the value increases by 25%." She paused for effect, or maybe because she realised she was slurring her words: "But that's not the point", still slurring, "The point is that gold is popular among people with a lot of undeclared cash income. If they cannot launder that cash, they also can't get a return on it. And the price of gold increased six-fold a couple of years back. Think about that, Marius. One million turned into six million. Stock market returns couldn't compete with that. White collar crooks and common criminals were clamouring for anything we could get our hands on, paying up to twice the market price."

I just could not believe that she would be able to spin a story like that in her drunken state if it wasn't true. I also knew that it was correct, gold had indeed increased dramatically in value a few years ago. "OK, Beatrice, I'll pay you that. Impressive. But you have to admit, it's quite sick that we both …"

She nodded her assent. What a pair, two ex smugglers, two half criminals. We were both crazy. Maybe that was our mutual turn-on. I thrust my hips up again, grabbed a breast with each hand, pulled her down. Then I whispered: "Do you remember the guy who fell into a manhole in Oslo a few weeks ago?"

She grabbed my shoulders, sat up and stared at me quizzically: "Yes ... was that you?" I nodded. "But why?"

"He was the one responsible for the damage to my knee." I told her the gist of the story of the failed smuggling attempt.

She shook her head in disbelief: "You won't believe it, Marius, this is totally sick, but I know him. Aron. Aron Tollefsen. Also known as 'the vise', alias 'the eel'. He bought gold barrels from me. For the money he wasn't able to launder through Torpedo Pizza. Three times. The last time he tried to deceive us. The man is a psychopath, Marius. I had to get some muscle brought in from Tokyo to sort it out. He won't ever touch me again."

We just stared at each other with wide eyes. She was still sitting on top of me, but the conversation had blown away the desire, my cock flaccid like wet cabbage. I was about to ask what Tokyo had to do with anything, but she beat me to it and asked: "So when your second smuggling attempt went bad, how did you get the money to pay Aron?"

That's when I realised that things were turning for the worse. A lot worse. I felt like I was sinking, but I was so addled with alcohol and my own accomplishments that I couldn't stop: "I witnessed a murder, Beatrice. By coincidence. So I blackmailed the killer, three million. I'm not proud of it, but I didn't have a choice. Aron would have destroyed me if I didn't pay up."

Again the incredulous looks at each other. The shit was piling up. I didn't know what to believe, our stories outdid each other. I tried an evasive manoeuvre, breaking away from her grip, to make a real fuck happening, but I couldn't move her. Instead she asked: "Who was killed, Marius? It would have to have been in the papers."

I hesitated, looking for an out that no longer existed,

resigned and said: "Steve Hall."

"What? she yelled out, gripped her own hair as if to hold on to something. "You know who killed Steve?"

"Hush, Beatrice, not so loud. We are not alone", I whispered and put a finger to my lips. "Yes, I do know who killed him."

Beatrice leaned forward, she was so close I could feel her breath: "Who?"

It felt like I had been hit by a fist to the face in slow motion. I had seen it coming, but was too stupid or too drunk to duck. And all just because I had needed to boast, to prove that I was a winner at any price. Maybe I subconsciously had wished to tell her that her father was a murderer … that I knew … if so I was about to have my wish fulfilled, trapped in my own net. I swallowed a couple of times before I whispered: "Your father."

Her mouth opened as if to scream, but no sound came out. Like Michael Corleone at the end of Godfather III, only her eyes were screaming. I lay completely still, without a clue as to what to do or what to expect. I could almost hear the cogs moving around in her head. At long last she asked me, her voice weak and shivering: "Are you sure, Marius?"

"Yes, Beatrice, I am sure. I was on the little island not far from your parents cottage when it happened. There was no wind. I heard almost everything that was said. Your mother was there. And Kai and Joe. Maybe more. But it was Gunnar who pulled the trigger."

"What the hell were you doing there?" she asked, having recovered the strength of her voice again.

"I was hiding from Aron."

"But why there? Why there of all places?"

"I had to get away from Oslo. Aron was after me. So I popped into an internet cafe and clicked Google Maps at random, away from Oslo, and that's where I ended up."

She shook her head, as if something had just been loosened in there. "But why? Why was Steve shot? He and dad were childhood friends."

"Steve Hall wanted to stop the Factory Outlet development. It was about money, as it always is." She nodded slowly, she was getting the picture. Not that hard when you had all the pieces of the puzzle. She seemed resigned rather than angry when she went on: "OK, Marius, I believe you. That dad was capable of murder … not all that unexpected, all things considered." Then she sat erect, still on top of me, her hands on her hips, suddenly sober: "but what I don't understand, Marius, is why are you here? Did you pick me up to get to dad? Is all this, our relationship, just a fucking charade?"

"No, Beatrice, absolutely not. You have to believe me, there is no connection. When I googled Gunnar to find out who he was, I found a photo of him, you and your mum on the homepage of Princess Yachts Owners Club. I recognised you from Business School, but I had no plans, no ulterior motives, on the night we met."

My throat was dry, I cleared my throat, before I continued: "How could I even know you were there? Our meeting just happened. You looked in my direction, twice, and you smiled at me. So I had to have a go. I knew you were Gunnar's daughter, that it was risky, but I still did it. That's just the way I am. And the fact that you, amongst all the potential suitors on the night, chose a cripple, I couldn't have guessed that. To be honest, I still don't quite get it."

As I talked, her eyes softened. "Cool, Marius, I get it", she said as she stroked my cheek. "I do believe you. Everything that's been said tonight is so sick that it's more likely to be true than not. For instance, neither of us would have known Aron if we lived normal lives." She got out of bed, pulled off my pants and my boxer-shorts, and sat back down, made herself comfortable.

But instead of the usual sensual foreplay - her languid, slow movements that eventually tensed me up like the bow of an arrow - she rode me fast and furious, and when we finished, she fell in a heap on top of me. When we regained our breath, I pushed her over on her side, put my arms around her and spooned her. I was almost asleep when I remembered what she had said earlier. It could, of course, wait until the morning, but I asked anyway: "Beatrice, what did you mean when you said you had to get the muscle from Tokyo to deal with Aron?"

It took a while, and I thought she might have fallen asleep, but then she said: "When I smuggled gold, I was working for some Japanese. I still do, but no longer with gold. I look after their directors and their major clients. For 20,000 a night."

Game On

Nothing more was said. Beatrice fell asleep in my arms, while I was shell-shocked trying to sort out what I thought. I had always been of the opinion that to be able to sell your body was a gift from God, the opportunity that women had when in desperate need to survive, like the very last piece of bread at the bottom of life's travel bag. And I had never looked down on prostitutes, quite the contrary, surmising that those choosing that path didn't have too many other options. But Beatrice did have options, she had a marketing degree and she was super smart. She could have done whatever she wanted, but for some reason she chose to sell her body. It was odd, but as I was lying there, pondering, I felt neither anger, nor jealousy, just a fear of losing her.

The situation felt somewhat different when I woke up around mid-morning. The hangover was moderate, only a mild headache and a dry mouth. The prostitution business didn't worry me. It was everything else. Beatrice now knew that I was a smuggler, a blackmailer and capable of inflicting physical harm on others. And I knew she was a smuggler and a prostitute. In that way we had something on each other, but I didn't know what that meant. What worried me most was her connection with Aron. One word, and I would be as good as dead.

Beatrice got out of bed and went to the bathroom. She came back wrapped in a towel and sat down at the end of the bed, feet curled up underneath. She tilted her head towards me and said with a croaky voice: "Well, Marius, that was some night. I wasn't sure if you'd still be here when I woke up, but here you are."

"I'm still here", I said reassuringly, throwing in a smile for good measure.

"The way I see it", she continued, her voice already more confident, "you have two alternatives. I charge 20,000 a night. So you either leave around 500,000 on the bedside table and walk away, or we continue as before."

"Do you take cards?" I said, before a pillow hit my head. We both laughed as I dragged her down next to me on the bed. We were facing each other, locking eyes. I told her of my simplistic view of women and their options, and that it didn't bother me, although I would prefer it was happening in London. That's how it was for me, out of sight, out of mind.

She stroked my cheek tenderly. I grabbed her hand and kissed it. The only thing I was curious about was why she was a prostitute, so I asked her. "Well, I suppose there is no secret that I am into sex. I have been since I was twelve years old, and there are no indications that it's about to change anytime soon. If that means I am a nymphomaniac, so be it, I don't give a shit about what other people think." She stared me down. I swallowed and nodded. "The decision to sell my body was made during a lesson in macroeconomics at Business School. The teacher, a slightly weird dude with ponytail and a distinct aquiline nose, was telling us about 'comparative advantages', that there were some absolute advantages, but everyone had an edge relative to others in one way or another. And that's when I understood that if I had an edge on anything in this life, it would be my body. From there, accepting the idea of making money having sex wasn't too much of a stretch."

She continued her story about how she had found her way into a bordello in Oslo, and in certain hotels, when she met this Japanese client. After just a weekend with her, he offered her a job in London, with her own apartment in fashionable Chelsea. There she'd receive well heeled Japanese businessmen for 2,000 pounds a night. The Japanese, she told me, were unbelievably formal and uptight, the social side was much more demanding than the sex, which was over very quickly in most cases. Many tipped her excessively afterwards, especially if they were allowed to take a photo of her white blond snatch. Then they would sneak out of her apartment, looking as if they were carrying pictures of the crucifixion of Jesus. It was easy money. She had set up a legitimate company, 'NOTA Analysis', invoicing the Japanese for market analysis services making it all look quite ordinary. She was even accumulating a pension.

After about a year, they had asked if she could be their Norwegian agent for gold transactions. That too was easy money, just a bit of organising, delivery and pick-ups. As she said in conclusion: "Why should I have to get up early to go to a job I'd dislike, when I can sleep in, have sex pretty much when it suits me, and make lots of money."

When I asked if she thought it was alright to have sex with just about anybody, she answered: "But that's the thing, Marius, it's not anybody. My London clients get it as a work bonus or as bribes, Japanese men representing their employers. They behave like choir boys. Occasionally I have other clients, but they pay me 20,000 of their own money. Most of them are both educated and well behaved. And many times it doesn't even involve sex, I'm just an escort. It's just not a problem." In the end I couldn't help myself: "But don't Japanese men have tiny willies?" She rolled her eyes and said that was a myth with no foundation in reality.

We had showered, packed our bags, just managed to grab what was left of the breakfast buffet and checked out. On the way back to town, Beatrice told me tidbits of what she thought about her father, now with the knowledge he was also a murderer. I think she was more shocked that Kai and Joe, most probably also someone named Peter, had been in on it. But after what her mother had told her, they had all made a fortune from the Factory Outlet development: Joe as the supplier of computer systems, Peter as a subcontractor and Kai as the General Manager on a very generous salary.

What she found most challenging was that her mother had kept quiet about it. They had often discussed what happened to Steve. He had been one of Vivian's suitors in her youth and had been a friend of the family. When I asked her what she'd do with her newly acquired knowledge, she answered without hesitation: "Tell the police."

"Maybe that's why your mum has kept quiet", I said, worried about my own involvement.

I was probably still above the limit, but that was nothing new. As we passed the Factory Outlet Stores, Beatrice pointed her index finger towards the centre and fired off a couple of imaginary shots. I asked her again: "Seriously, Beatrice, what will you do?"

She went quiet, used the nail on one finger to push back her cuticles, one by one, examined the result, before answering: "I just think he should rot away in jail." She continued the manicure.

"But what about all the others that would be dragged into the maelstrom? Your mother, Joe and the others? What about your father's company and the employees?"

She chuckled, before answering: "And what about you, Marius? Are you not also afraid for your own skin?"

"Sure", I said, "I'll admit that. If an investigation is opened on Gunnar, there's no telling what they'll uncover. There is an email on Gunnar's PC which is from me. I am guessing that the police would be able to find out where it originates from, and then I'll have some explaining to do."

She went quiet again, looked out the car window for a while, before saying: "The only two people I care about are you and mum. I don't know the punishment for failing to report a murder, but it won't be pleasant. So I get that."

Phew, I felt relieved, thinking this would sort itself out

somehow.

Then she said: "What if we do another round on dad, blackmail him again for even more money?"

The thought hadn't even occurred to me, I had put it all behind me. The furniture business was going gangbusters, and I had the flexibility and the financial freedom to do more or less what I wanted. Content with life as it was. So all I could muster was a hesitant: "Yeah?"

"Don't you get it, Marius. The only thing that matters to dad is money. Money and status. We can get him where it hurts the most."

I could tell by her voice that she was getting excited by the idea, likely as much for the murky past as for somehow avenging Steve Hall. There would be no way back now, so I asked: "What do you reckon he is worth?"

"According to mum he got around 35 million for the sale of the land after it had been re-regulated for commercial usage."

"And since then he has bought a boat for ten million. What about the rest? In the bank, or invested in something?"

"He is a part-owner of the Factory Outlet Stores, so I believe most of it is there."

"In other words", I concluded, "he may not be all that liquid. That makes it more difficult, although that's the point. How much did you have in mind?"

"How about 35 million? Divided in half. We are partners, just like 'Bonnie and Clyde'. 17.5 million each is not to sneeze at." A wide, greedy smile spread across her face.

"That won't work, Beatrice. That's just not possible. Even the very wealthy couldn't get away with that, the white collar crime unit would be on to it in a flash."

"So what? Then he gets what he deserves."

"Yes, that's true. But we'll get nothing. And if he folds under the pressure, it's all over. Then all hell breaks loose."

"Hmm", she demurred, her lips clasped together. "What do

you reckon? How much could he manage to fork up?"

"Maybe five million. It doesn't sound that much, but it's a lot of cash. Can't see how he'd manage more. He'd have to sell the new boat, with some of it under the table."

"Fantastic. Mum tells me he acts like a buffoon on the fly-bridge. Refusing to acknowledge anyone on boats less than 40 feet."

"Perfect, how good is that! Let's fleece him just enough so all he can afford is a Princess 39. Then he'll have real self-esteem issues!" We had a chuckle at that. We were in good spirits.

Strangely, I always felt extra calm in the twilight zone on the way down from a drunken high. I could feel poetic, observing nuances I otherwise wouldn't notice, often becoming very talkative, breaking into long dissertations about almost nothing, to the great consternation of those around me. It was a dangerous trait for those more than usually fond of the amber liquids, enjoying the hangover. I looked at Beatrice, would have loved to know what she was thinking, but she looked content at least. I had another thought: "But, Beatrice, if we blackmail Gunnar, aren't you stealing from yourself? All you are getting is your inheritance in advance, but I get half of it."

She looked puzzled, before responding: "No, I don't believe so. Gunnar threatened to cut me out of the will a few years ago. If he has legally done that already, I don't know."

"Wow. What happened?"

She smiled: "It was quite ridiculous. It happened while I was still working in Oslo. I would pick up some of my clients at the bar at the Continental Hotel. This particular evening I had hooked an American who was staying at the hotel. Leaving his room at about 3am, I ran into dad with a prostitute on their way to a room. We just stopped and stared at each other, not a word was said and then we kept going in opposite directions."

"Seriously?"

"Yes, Marius, that's the truth. The next time we met he told me he would disinherit me, that no whore would be spending his money."

"But what the fuck, he was caught out with his pants down, so to speak. That's just two sides of the same coin."

"Exactly. But that's the way he is. He has an amazing ability to block out any other vantage points than his own. He should have been a lawyer."

It was a bizarre situation, father and daughter. "But what about your mother? What did she know?"

"I told her what I was doing from the beginning. She didn't like it much, but she accepted it as my choice. When I told her about the meeting at The Continental, she said she had suspected that he was being unfaithful, but she didn't care anymore. It meant she didn't need to have sex with him."

"And still she stays?"

"Yes, that's just the way it is. But truth be told, mum has her own secrets. So maybe it meant they were even." After a couple of seconds she continued: "yes, Marius, welcome to the family. Do you still want to marry me?" She laughed out loud, before saying: "And just to complete the picture, guess who mum had an affair with?"

Who could it be? I was about to say Joe, just for fun, but then I had an inkling: "Steve Hall?"

She nodded.

Fuck it. It almost defied belief. "Do you think…"

"I don't know. Don't think he knew. But it's possible. Two birds with one stone."

Again, we drifted into our own thoughts. If we were going to squeeze Gunnar for money, how would we go about it? Now he knew what I looked like. On the other hand there were now two of us. But it would be hard to organise a transfer without physically meeting. That's as far as I got in my ruminations, before Beatrice exclaimed: "gold!"

"What?" I asked, confused.

"It's not illegal to buy gold. Don't you get it? We can get dad to buy gold, it's totally legal. He can buy as much as he likes. I want a Monster Box. And you shall have one, too."

"Huh, what's a Monster Box?"

Beatrice was beyond excited as she explained:

"A Monster Box is a box containing 500 Canadian Maple Leafs 24 carat gold coins, each weighing one ounce, or 31.1 grams. The price today is around 8,500 per ounce, so a Monster Box will cost approximately 4.5 million. Two, we have to have one each, nine million."

"But what will we do with the gold?"

"Gold, Marius, gold is awesome. To hold a plastic tube containing ten gold coins is indescribable. It weighs just 310 grams, but is worth 85,000. And it's easy to turn over. All you need is to walk into any reputable jeweller or coin collector store anywhere in the world and cash out at around 95% of the spot price. No questions asked. Go on holiday and bring three or four coins in your wallet, there is your 30,000 spending money!"

I had to admit it didn't seem like such a bad idea. "OK", I started, "but I still don't get why gold is easier than cash?"

Beatrice smiled knowingly, before she said: "A bit slow today, Marius? It's because Gunnar can buy as much gold as he wants, totally legal, just like investing in shares."

"So he could buy nine million in gold without anyone taking any notice?"

"Well, someone might notice it, but it's completely legal. Oslo is too small a market to handle a volume like that, so he'll have to travel to London or Frankfurt. Once there, he buys two Monster Boxes, payable on delivery, he brings it back to Oslo, puts them in a bank safety box. So now, instead of having nine million in cash, he has nine million in gold, which he declares on his tax return as an asset. The point is, we remove the gold from the deposit box, so it's empty. As long as dad has a receipt for the purchase, the tax man won't check the box. And as a bonus, he'll have to pay asset tax on that gold every year thereafter, for an asset he no longer owns." Again that laugh, laced with malice. "Think about that, Marius, dad who hates to pay tax. It'll annoy him so much he'll have a stroke."

It was starting to sink in, and I couldn't see any obvious weakness. "OK, Beatrice, I'll buy that. Well thought out. But how are we going to get hold of the gold? Neither of us can risk being seen by Gunnar, of course. by the way, what's the weight of a Monster Box?"

"One box is almost 16 kilos, so that's just above 30 kilos in total. And not much in volume, so that should be manageable."

"Yes, that can be carried, but not so easily if you have to make a runner."

"You're right, Marius, and especially in your case."

"So we'll have to find a way of getting the gold without having to meet Gunnar face to face and without having to be in a hurry. So there's a challenge."

"Definitely", she yawned, as she stretched out and folded her seat back as far as it would go and closed her eyes. "You think about that, Marius, while I examine the inside of my eyelids for a while. After all, you need to earn your 4.5 million."

I glanced at her, she had moved on her side, her legs tucked up, hands between her thighs. She looked like a mermaid. And if my memory was correct, mermaids were omens of stormy weather and shipwrecks. It was going to be a perilous autumn.

~ ~ ~

The next couple of weeks were busy, Beatrice went to London a couple of times, and I had eight container-loads of imported furniture to attend to. Except for missing her when she was gone, I felt no jealousy. Work was work.

The planning of 'Operation Gold' was happening in fits and starts. Beatrice had found a dealer in London. Gunnar would have to pay 20% on signing the contract, the balance the day before dispatch. The gold would be handed to a courier who'd take it on a plane to Oslo Airport. Armaguard would take control as soon as the plane landed, delivering it to Gunnar, or to the bank, depending on what was agreed. That was the easy part. The tricky part was how to get our hands on the gold afterwards. We considered everything from using a speedboat to a make-shift cable-way across a railway track, but in the end we ended up with a plan involving a taxi. The plan was tested according to Persian rules and it passed muster with ease. The only things we needed were a mobile that couldn't be tracked, and some inside information from the traffic management authority. Beatrice assured me that she'd take care of both.

One month to the day after Gunnar' and Vivian's birthday party, Beatrice and I sat down at a cafe with WiFi. I logged into the old email account, 'isawyoumate@gmail.com', and started typing: "Hi Gunnar, remember me? Since we last spoke I can see that you have made a lot of money, but I have spent mine. To be fair, I think it's your job to do something about that. So let's play a game. To participate, you'll first need two million, and a few days later, another eight million. The good news is that the game will be played in accordance with the Norwegian regulations for customs duties and tax. When you have raised the money, you'll need to log in to gold.stock.uk and place an order for two Monster Boxes of Canadian Leaf gold coins. If you handle the negotiations of commissions, insurance and transport well, you might even have some money left over. The rest is easy. You have ten days from now to place the order, at which time you'll need the initial two million. The balance is payable upon delivery. If you don't want to, or you can't play the game, you lose. Then I'll send a letter to The World and to the police with a suggestion to check the connection between the murder of Steve Hall, the Factory

Outlet Stores and you. You have 48 hours to accept. If you want to play, just reply 'OK' and maybe a smiley face. If I haven't heard anything by the deadline, I win on a walk-over. And like the last time, Gunnar, this is all non-negotiable." Then I wrote in the subject line: "STEVE HALL IS STILL DEAD." I looked at Beatrice. She was almost ready to giggle.

"Well said, Marius. I think he'll fret as much about how it's written as he will about the content. He just cannot handle being treated like a fool." She grinned, showing all her teeth, she didn't seem to have any qualms about blackmailing her own father.

I grabbed her index finger and put it next to mine, then I kissed her on the mouth, just as we hit enter. Game on.

Monster Boxes

As usual, Gunnar was sitting at the Red Goat Cafe going through the morning's email. They had a fancy new coffee machine at work, but for one reason or another, it didn't quite match the coffee at Red Goat. Maybe it was just the blend of coffee. Business was good, and even though the rest of Europe was in the throes of a recession, the backlog of orders at his company was impressive. Sealing concrete had more to do with global warming and the vagaries of weather than the state of the economy. Not to mention the council building authorities' often lackadaisical approval processes for residential and commercial building projects in flood exposed areas. Gunnar had every reason to feel smug. He was halfway through the unread emails, his eyes scanned the list for anything interesting when he saw the subject line in capital letters: "STEVE HALL IS STILL DEAD." He recognised the sender, too. Without even looking at it, he flung the paper-cup against the wall. After three years of email phobia, he had finally started to relax, to the point where he believed that the case was dead and buried. His index finger shaking, he clicked to open.

Twelve hours later, Gunnar, Joe, Kai and Peter were seated around the boardroom table in Gunnar's office. They had been summoned as if called up for military service. None of the conscripted soldiers had any idea what it was about. Until now. They were all reading the email from isawyoumate@gmail.com. Gunnar watched them closely. He was still not quite convinced that the blackmailer was not someone from his social circle. There was something about how the email was framed which made it appear too personal to have been written by a complete stranger, without him being able to put his finger on exactly what it was. He could almost believe it was Joe, the most timid among them. Precisely because the arrogant tone of the email would point in every other direction but him. Even if Joe could appear obtuse in a lot of situations, he was very clever with computers and electronics. Could this contradiction hide another side to him? Gunnar glanced in his direction. Could it really be Joe?

It was Kai who broke the silence. "I knew it. We said it three years ago, too. You remember? You'll never be rid of him. He'll squeeze you until you are on the street in nothing but undies".

Peter continued: "Yes, it's not such a huge surprise. But what strikes me is why now? You sold your land two-three years ago. Why did he wait this long?"

Kai answered: "Because he's run out of money. He says that straight out. He's used one million a year, and now he wants more. If he continues like that, you'll be off the hook for the next ten years. Maybe not so bad, a million a year."

"What if he's bluffing?" Joe intoned. Gunnar pricked his ears up. What a good question to ask if it was him who was behind it, the perfect double bluff. Joe had made good money from the Factory Outlet Stores, having delivered all the cabling, the hardware and much of the software. Bought himself an SUV worth over a million and been on a three week luxury holiday to Thailand with his wife. Much wants more. Just the mere possibility that someone close to him could be behind this, made Gunnar see red.

Or what was it Peter had just said: Why now? Peter was very perceptive, he had more common sense than the other two put together. Had something happened recently that had made the blackmailing bastard try again? Not something he could come up with right now, but in need of further consideration.

Gunnar put both hands on the table, palms up, to accentuate the message. "I don't know, boys. I don't know anything you don't know. Of course there is the possibility that he *is* bluffing. Is anyone prepared to take that risk? Should we just ignore the email and see what happens?"

Gunnar looked around the table. Peter met his gaze, the other two wavered.

"Don't start that discussion again, Gunnar", said Peter with venom. "It was you who shot Steve. This is your responsibility, and yours alone. We helped you the last time. No fucking way I'm doing it again."

Gunnar glared at Joe and Kai, still without making eye contact. Then he said: "So this is what I get, boys. You have all made millions from the Factory Outlet, solely because of me. Do you think it's been easy? Don't you think it's been giving me grief every bloody day. What about your fancy cars? Trips to Thailand and Dubai?" Gunnar was seething inside, but he knew he couldn't let it get to him. Then he'd be left by himself. He continued: "Yes, maybe I should do just that, take the chance that he is bluffing. What then? Either nothing happens, and everything goes on like before. Or it all falls apart. I'll be charged with the murder. But the police and the press will no doubt start looking into how much you've all made on what happened. Then they'll ask why you didn't come forward at the time?"

They were quiet, not even Peter had anything to say to that.

"Exactly", Gunnar said, "that's what I thought. So don't pretend you are all innocent. If I'm going to hell, then I'll make damn sure I get some company at least part of the way."

Nobody said anything. After an uncomfortably long pause, Kai said: "But, I don't get it, what's the thing with the Monster Boxes?"

"He wants gold", Gunnar said. "I have been on the internet all day. A Monster Box contains 500 gold coins. Unfortunately, this guy is quite clever. Ten million in cash would have been almost impossible to raise, and he understands that, but buying gold for ten million is quite straightforward."

"So are you going to pay?" Peter said.

"If nobody has any ingenious suggestions, I don't think we have a choice. I don't believe he's bluffing. He did have a gun the last time. The point this time is to find out who he is. And then we hit back. Recover the gold and get rid of him. He's pressing us for a small fortune, he is mocking us, making a laughing stock out of us. If he wants to take us on, he better beware."

Kai and Joe started talking at the same time. Kai said: "That's what you said the last time, we'd find him and get our money back."

"Are you going to kill him, too?" Joe asked.

Again, Gunnar had trouble staying in control: "For fuck's sake boys. Do you think this is a bloody game? He's about to crush us. We either pay up, or he'll ruin our lives. If I have to do this by myself, and get caught, you'd better believe that I'll take you all down with me. I'll say that the murder of Steve was planned and that you were in on it from the outset." Gunnar stood up, legs apart, hands on hips, ready to defend himself. "I'm serious, if you let me down, you'll join me in the gutter."

Once more the room went quiet. After another long pause, Peter spoke: "Gunnar, go for a walk. Give us five minutes. It has to be all of us or nothing." Gunnar slammed the door as he left the room.

15 minutes later Gunnar was called back to the boardroom. Too worked up to sit down, he stood leaning against the wall, arms crossed. Peter was taking the lead: "We just cannot accept this type of blackmail, Gunnar. You are no better than this guy. But we are willing to hear what you have to say if you sign this confession, stating that you, and you alone, were responsible for the murder of Steve, both in planning and in execution. If you won't sign it, we'll all walk out."

Gunnar took one look at the piece of paper, sighed and

said: "OK. I apologise for what I said, but I'm desperate. I can't do it by myself. And we have to end it." He sat down and continued: "If you all contribute one million each, I'll take care of the balance, roughly six million. That I can manage. And it's all legal. I'll take care of formalities." Gunnar could have managed the whole amount by himself, but he wanted them on board, to make sure they were all motivated. He couldn't help himself glancing at Joe one more time, but didn't pick up any clues. Gunnar went on: "But I'm not prepared to be deceived yet again. Giving away nine million in gold. No fucking way. This time we'll get him."

Peter nodded towards Kai and Joe: "Alright, Gunnar, give us another five." Gunnar left the room, this time without slamming the door.

It took them more than 15 minutes, but in the end they had all agreed. Again Peter was their spokesperson: "OK, Gunnar, we are all in, provided you sign here."

Gunnar grabbed a pen and signed.

~ ~ ~

47 hours and 30 minutes after we had sent the email to Gunnar, Beatrice and I were at a cafe not far from my apartment. Still no reply. I bet a five-star restaurant dinner that we'd hear something within the next half hour. Beatrice took the bet, always ready to counter in the interest of fun and games. I was unsure what her main motivation was, revenge or greed. It wouldn't surprise me if she'd take the gold, and then tip off the police anyway. She was, as I had learnt by now, a typical 'having it both ways' kind of girl, not unlike myself, come to think of it. Three minutes before time was up, we had the confirmation: "OK." But no smileys.

~ ~ ~

Once again, Gunnar was sitting in the boardroom waiting.

He had used most of his available liquidity, as well as borrowed three million from his own company, to make it happen. The transaction with gold.stock.uk had been carried out without a hitch, and two grey boxes, the so called Monster Boxes, were on the table in front of him. Each box slightly larger than a one kilo packet of wheat flour, each box weighing about 16 kilos, each box worth an incredible 4.6 million. The gold coins were packed in small plastic cylinders, ten coins in each, fifty cylinders in each box. The email he had received from the blackmailer had been printed out and four copies placed around the table. Gunnar picked up his own copy and read through it for the umpteenth time:

"Hi Gunnar, this is what I want you to do: Package each of the Monster Boxes in a wooden crate of 40x50x60 cm and fill it up with Styrofoam chips. This coming Thursday, on the 14th, bring both boxes to the Coffee Brewery cafe at 2:30pm. Have a cup of coffee. Within one hour you will be contacted by Mr Bojangles. Hand over the boxes to him and do not leave for another 15 minutes. If you do, or if anybody tries to get in his way, or follow Mr Bojangles afterwards, or if I find any tracking devices in any of the boxes, I keep the gold, and I have set up an email to be sent at 7pm to The World and to the police, and the rest will run its course. Good luck. PS: I see you, but you can't see me". Gunnar looked at his watch. He removed 36 of the plastic tubes and placed twelve of them on top of each of the other copies of the email.

The boys had bought gold for one million each, 120 coins, 3.7 kg. He wanted them to feel what it was like to handle real gold, a feeling that had made kings and popes lose their heads throughout history, a feeling Gunnar knew he was not immune from, either. Hopefully, that would be enough motivation for all of them to do whatever it would take.

They arrived together as usual, showing that they represented a united front, all of them equally sombre. But even before they sat down, or read the email, they started fondling the containers, opening them and pouring the gold coins on the table, fascinated by their weight and shine. They seemed very motivated.

Kai was the first to comment on the email: "What's he up to this time, I wonder? Mr Bojangles? I don't understand?"

Gunnar shook his head slowly: "Who knows. But I think we should be prepared for almost anything."

"Unless that's exactly what he is counting on", Peter speculated, "for us to believe that something unexpected is going to happen, but in reality a man introducing himself as Mr Bojangles is simply going to pick up the boxes and drive away."

"Or does it have something to do with Sammy Davis, Jr., maybe a black man?" Kai said.

"Or is he just mocking us again, Mr Bojangles dancing away from us?"

"That's it, exactly", Gunnar said, "it can mean anything or nothing. We can be certain that his name is not Bojangles though. And Sammy Davis Jr. is dead, isn't he?"

"The starting point is that I'll have to be at the Coffee Brewery next Thursday at 2:30pm, with the gold in two boxes."

"Where is that?" Kai asked.

"Not far from here. Unlikely that's a coincidence. It's open, accessible, lots of glass. Easy for him to see what is happening if he's around. But that will also give us a chance to get a glimpse of him. Works both ways."

"But if Mr Bojangles is going to pick up the boxes, and he is somewhere else observing it, then he would have other people involved. That doesn't sound good." Peter looked at Gunnar with concern.

"Yes and no", Gunnar responded. "We can't be sure that he has told Mr Bojangles what it's about. All he knows is that he is picking up two boxes. That's most likely why he has asked us to repackage them, so that the weight is not going to give the content away. At the same time it gives us a chance to observe this person, and he must have some sort of association with the blackmailer."

"But how are we going to be able to follow the car and the boxes?" Kai asked. "He will no doubt scrutinise the boxes for any signs of tracking devices. Or he'll get rid of the packaging, like he did the last time."

Gunnar smiled. He had been looking forward to this moment. He reached under the table and brought out a plastic box which had been sitting on a chair next to him. He opened it, held up something looking like a pistol, large calibre, but with a short barrel. "With this", he said, pulled back the breech, pointed towards a window and fired. All they heard was a faint "pop" and that was it. They looked at him inquisitively. "Come have a look", Gunnar stood up and walked towards the window. "There", he was pointing at a speck on the glass.

Inside a small, flat lump of transparent jelly was a tiny piece of metal, no larger than the head of a pin. Kai tried to prod it loose, to no avail. It's stuck there, Gunnar said categorically, "it sticks to everything. You'll need a razor blade to get it off." Gunnar returned to his chair and opened an iPad that was sitting on the table in front of him, and said: "Look here, boys", after a few seconds a map appeared on the screen, with a tiny blinking cursor. "There", Gunnar said with satisfaction.

"Are you saying that there is a transmitter in that tiny little piece of jelly?" Peter asked with astonishment.

"Yes", Gunnar said. "Transmits for at least six hours. it's activated by the shock of the gunshot. The jelly is the battery."

Gunnar reached for the pistol. "This is a 'gum gun', the latest in surveillance from USA."

"So what exactly are you planning?" Kai asked, obviously impressed.

"We do what we have been told to do. I'll sit down at the cafe at 2:30 and wait. They'll have to come by car. I can't see him picking up the two cases, strolling along the pavement and onto the train. He'll be parked right outside, quick to get inside, and a quick departure. Peter, you'd be the best shot, so that'll be your job. Park on the other side of the street. When you see what's happening, roll down your window, point and shoot a 'gum' at the door or the boot of the car. It sticks, even on a wet car covered in dirt."

"But what if they don't park right outside? What if there are no parking spots there?" Peter asked.

"There is plenty of room to double park there for a few minutes. People do it all the time. But if against expectation he should park somewhere else, you have to get out of the car and follow on foot. There are only two ways out of the area, so they'll have to pass you. When they do, you lift your coat and point the 'gun' towards the side somewhere. As you heard, it doesn't make much noise when it hits, and from inside the car you can't hear a thing. That's the whole point."

"And then what?" Joe asked carefully. Gunnar couldn't quite get rid of his suspicion of Joe's involvement. Maybe he had been blabbering to someone when he was drunk, he was always more talkative then, and maybe it was Mr Bojangles who controlled the whole thing. With Joe as the insider, now privy to everything they needed to know. Joe could maybe also have the means to track down the owner of isawyoumate@gmail.com, even if he claimed it could not be done. Now that would be as shrewd as shrewd could be. But for now, he'd have to ignore that possibility.

"Furthermore, I'll have to stay for 15 minutes. But you will be able to track the car. I want Joe and Peter in one car with the iPad, and Joe by himself in another car. We establish a conference call so everyone can follow. I'll get a Bluetooth headset for everyone. Stay behind at a safe distance, there is no reason to take any chances."

"Why am I always the one to be by myself?" Joe asked,

despondent.

"Same reason as the last time, Joe. If we need someone to get out and see what's happening, you are the least conspicuous looking. Then Kai and Joe can direct you, you can park and walk around. It's the best way", Gunnar said with finality, pleased that Joe was somewhat sidelined.

"And what then?", Peter said, "what do we do when they stop? If it's not Mr Bojangles who is the blackmailer, it's likely he'll go to meet him somewhere. What then?"

"Either way, we can't do anything straight away. The email is timed for 7pm. Our purpose is to gather information. The type of car, registration number, places. Bring a camera and use it when you can. Everything we can get hold of. If we can do that, then I'll take care of the rest. Believe me, I want our gold back."

Gunnar picked up one of the tubes and let the coins roll into his cupped hands, shaking to hear the hollow, clunking sound. There were 700 coins in the pot, there was no fucking way the blackmailing punk was going to get the better of him this time around.

Mr Bojangles

We would have managed just fine, Beatrice and I, but I still decided to include Brad. Beatrice had been wary of involving an outsider, but I argued that we needed an extra pair of eyes on Gunnar at the start, and told her I trusted Brad with my life. In addition, Brad already knew the whole story.

For her part, Beatrice had delivered on her promises: a prepaid mobile, most likely stolen, and some inside information from the Road Traffic Authority. That woman had contacts everywhere. At this moment she was standing at a junction critical to our plans, wearing a beanie, a scarf and a long coat, more fcamouflage than to keep warm.

I was in the parking lot of the Kolbotten shopping centre, a very large, multi-level mall, southeast of Oslo, about 30 minutes by car from the Coffee Brewery. I had been calling the Oslo Taxi line at regular intervals over the last hour, just to hang up as soon as I got through. The current waiting time was about five minutes. No worries there. It was 2:15. Time to get started. I dialled the number again and waited.

After about seven minutes I got through: "Oslo Taxi, your pickup address, please?" a friendly sounding female voice.
"Hi there", I said, in my most amiable tone, "I have a small problem I was hoping you could help me with."
"I'll try", she said sounding accommodating. I envisaged her as a pleasant, good humoured and kind lady in her late thirties, a bit on the heavy side, but still attractive; but also aware that women with the sweetest voices could as likely be fat fifty-somethings with grey hair and yellow teeth.
I continued: "A mate of mine is sitting at the Coffee Brewery over on the other side of town with two wooden crates that I urgently need to get hold of. I am in the Kolbotten

shopping centre car-park. Could you organise a taxi to pick them up and drive them to me here, please?"

"Sure, we can do that. What's the name?"

"My name is Samuel Davids."

"And how will the driver find your friend at the Coffee Brewery?"

"He is sitting there with these two crates. All the driver needs to do is to tell him his name is Mr Bojangles and that he is picking up the two crates, that's just a code we use."

"One of my favourite songs", she said with a chuckle.

"Mine, too", I said.

"No worries at all", she said, "you'd even be saving some money as there is no sales tax on the transport of goods. You'll get a text message with the confirmation within a few minutes."

"Thanks so much, great service, you are an angel", I said and finished the conversation. First move made, white pawn to D4.

~ ~ ~

Gunnar sat down on one of the bar-stools facing the window, one foot on the top of the two crates stacked on the floor in front of him. The floor to ceiling glass provided the perfect view of everyone coming and going. The cafe was half full, mostly with the upwardly mobile set, young men and women with what Gunnar considered unrealistic ambitions, young mothers with prams, and some not as easily categorised. For some reason, the music playing was rather loud Italian opera, as if trying to give the cafe some extra kudos. Kai had parked his BMW diagonally across the road. He could just make him out behind a newspaper in the front seat, but the dark tinted glass hid Peter from view in the back seat. But he was there, Gunnar knew, gum gun ready. Joe was parked a bit further down, pointing in the opposite direction.

Somewhere there would likely be a guy observing him. He

could well be the bald man sitting next to him, with the Tom Ford glasses, reading the Financial Times. Or one of the mothers, for that matter. Or the person standing on the roof of the office building over the road, smoking a cigarette.

Or … Gunnar looked over at the building and noticed that both the top floors seemed like they were empty, no lights and naked walls. Some windows had the outside blinds down, others up. Why had he not noticed that before? That was definitely why he had chosen the Coffee Brewery as the handover location. As he had written: "I see you, but you can't see me." Gunnar was tempted to run across the road, find him, and beat the living daylights out of him, but with the email set to send automatically at 7pm, he knew he couldn't take that risk. But it triggered an idea.

At 2:38pm a taxi stopped right outside, a yellow Mercedes station wagon, the most common of Oslo taxis. A taxi? Could that be it? "There's a taxi outside, watch out", Gunnar said calmly into the Bluetooth headset. The taxi turned on the hazards and the driver came out. Gunnar thought it was probably a weary driver in need of a caffeine hit. As he came inside, he looked around, spotted Gunnar, and walked right up to him. "I am Mr Bojangles, he said with a slightly awkward smile", the pronunciation not sounding quite right, "and those are the crates I am picking up?", pointing at them.

"Er, yes, that'd be right", Gunnar said, unsure of what that actually meant. Was he going to hand over nine million in gold to a taxi driver? Or was it the blackmailer himself who was standing in front of him?

"Do I need to sign something? Is there a receipt or a consignment note?" The driver was acting professionally. If he had known the situation or what was in the crates, he would not have been so calm. In other words, this was an outsider, an uninitiated middle-man.

"No, no paperwork." Gunnar was thinking furiously, and then he asked: "What's the delivery address?" The driver looked at him strangely. Maybe not so odd. The crates could be full of illicit drugs. "You see", said Gunnar, "I was just asked to be here and wait for someone to pick them up. that's all."

"The parking lot at the Kolbotten Shopping Centre. To a mister Samuel Davies."

"OK", said Gunnar, relieved that the driver didn't make a fuss about his question. "The crates are rather heavy. So let's grab one each", Gunnar said, and lifted up the top one. At that moment he heard Peter say "taxi hit, rear right door." The driver took the other crate and they followed each other outside towards the taxi. Gunnar considered asking who had booked the taxi, but thought better of it. They now had the car tracked and they knew where it was going. That had to count for something.

"Drive safely", Gunnar said as they put the crates in the boot. The taxi did a u-turn and headed for the ring-road. "Did you get the delivery address, boys, the parking lot at the Kolbotten Shopping Centre. Follow three or four cars behind. Do you have him on the iPad, Peter?"

"Yes, under control."

"Good. I have to stay in the cafe for 15 minutes longer. Let's keep the lines open. Are you with us, Joe?"

"I am here", he said, pointedly.

~ ~ ~

Einstein was right, time is relative. I was counting the seconds and got to 70 in most cases before the minute hand on the large wall clock shifted once every minute. And five minutes lasted much longer than five minutes in Kiefer Sutherland's world of the TV series '24', which lasted only two or three minutes.

At last I was interrupted by the sound of "Sail away with me honey", a personalised ringtone Brad had programmed on my phone: "Elvis has just left the building", he started, in a passable Tennessee drawl. "They have loaded the crates into a yellow Mercedes station wagon, taxi no. A-1208. And I can inform you that Gunnar is wearing a Bluetooth headset, so I am guessing he has some communication happening. Be careful. Anything else?"

"Check if the taxi is being followed. He is bound to try something."

"Let's see. The taxi is doing a u-turn, and so is a white BMW X5, a u-turn and following. Registration AK something. Didn't get the rest. But it didn't look coincidental."

"Great, Brad. Thank you. Just leave when it feels natural. I'll be in touch." I allowed myself a slight smile, so far so good. I picked up the stolen mobile phone and called the taxi number again, on hold whilst calling Beatrice on my own phone. Beatrice answered on the first ring: "What's up", she said, feigning a yawn, as if she was bored.

"What's up", I said, with a lot more enthusiasm. "is that a yellow Mercedes station wagon taxi, no. A-1208, is on its way towards you. Shouldn't be hard to spot, followed in all likelihood by a white BMW X5. How is traffic?"

"it's starting to clog up. Looking good. The police have already pulled over four or five cars."

"Excellent. I reckon you'll see them in ten or fifteen minutes. Keep it up, Beatrice, nobody will be able to say we didn't work hard for our pot of gold!"

I was about to elaborate with what we were making per hour, but on the other phone a voice came through: "Oslo Taxi, how can I help you?", the voice a lot deeper than the earlier, cheerful one.

"Hi", I said, as I dropped my mobile into my lap, "this is Samuel Davies. I just ordered a taxi to come to the parking lot at the Kolbotten Shopping Centre, but I have had to move. So could I ask you to contact the driver and ask him to meet me at the main entrance, around the block from the parking area, instead. I'll be standing outside."

"What's the taxi number?" the man asked in a terse voice.

"Ah yes, of course, he-he", I answered, "how would you know, it's not like there is only one taxi out and about, is it? It's taxi no. A-1208."

"No worries. I'll call the driver and give him the new destination. Have a nice day", he said and hung up.

I picked up my own phone from my lap and asked: "Are you still there, Beatrice?"

She laughed: "Very impressive, Marius. If the rest of the day goes as well as that telephone conversation I might as well quit."

"It's going pretty well so far", I said. "Just wait and see. Call me when you see them", I finished and hung up. It was paramount that I did. To stay focused. With nine million in gold at stake, it would be ludicrous to be distracted, a common occurrence during extended conversations with Beatrice.

~ ~ ~

Gunnar looked at this watch. 15 minutes. He had resolved to drive towards his office, and then turn around and come back. If anybody had been hiding behind the blinds in the building opposite, he would have most likely parked his car in the basement car-park of the building. Gunnar found the stairwell at the back, and took up a position where he could see everyone entering the car-park.

He saw a woman. Middle aged, dressed in business attire. Went straight to her car, got in and started driving. Unlikely. Gunnar didn't even make a note of the registration number. Then a younger man. Athletic, broad shoulders, with a backpack. What was in the backpack? Maybe binoculars? The man walked sprightly towards a Jeep, got inside and started texting on his mobile. Ah well, messaging someone before leaving?

Gunnar got his pen out and a piece of paper from his

wallet, ready to take down the registration number, when he heard Peter's voice reverberating in his ear: "FUCK. NOT NOW. KEEP DRIVING, KAI, KEEP DRIVING!"

"What's happening?" Gunnar yelled back.

"We are fuckin' being waved over by the police. They are pulling over ineligible drivers in the bus-lane. The taxi got in the lane, and we followed."

"Joe", Gunnar shouted, "get out of the bus-lane."

"I never got in" Joe said from his car.

"Where is the taxi? Can you see it?" Gunnar continued anxiously.

"I can see it, but it's a fair way ahead, past the service station." Fuck this. We are queued up here, too. There are four cars ahead of us waiting to be fined, or whatever you get for driving in the bus-lane. This is not working. I'll get out and see what I can do."

"How are you going, Joe" Gunnar was trying to keep calm, knowing they were at a critical juncture, but he wasn't succeeding.

"Traffic is moving OK. I'm past the pedestrian walk-way, going towards the tunnel, I can see Kai's car to my right. Should I get into the bus-lane or to the service station?"

"What the hell, Joe, you have to hang on to the taxi as if your life depended on it."

"Excuse me", Gunnar heard Peter say, "we are already late for a very important meeting. It's very serious, many jobs at stake. Could you please write out the fine, so we can keep going?"

"Get back in your car", Gunnar could hear a stern voice in the background.

"But we haven't got time", Peter pleaded, without being able to hide his anger.

"Get back in your car", the constable said, this time his voice threatening.

"But…"

"Get back!" This time there was no doubt. The next utterance would have consequences.

"Fucking hell", Peter yelled out as he got back in the car. "We'll lose him. This will take time."

"Calm down, boys", Gunnar said in a voice that masked how stressed he was, "this is not the time to lose our heads. We know where he's going. We have him tracked. Joe might be four or five minutes behind him. If I remember correctly, there is no bus-lane on the other side of the tunnel, due to roadworks. Keep Joe informed, Peter, and then Joe should be able to catch up in time. "But the worst part is that he planned this. He has fucking deceived us again!"

~ ~ ~

The phone rang again. This time it was 'These boots are made for walking', by Nancy Sinatra, which Beatrice had entered as her ringtone. She had read that the song had been used by the CIA as a way of terrorising a dictator to get out of an embassy in Panama. Therefore quite fitting for Beatrice, with the subtext: "one of these days, these boots are gonna walk all over you".

"The taxi went past ten seconds ago", she said excitedly, "and a white BMW X5 was just waved in. Registration is AK30393. Send a text to 2282, and we'll find out who owns it."

I entered the registration number to the Motor Vehicle Authority, yet another example of how privacy was yielding to citizen protection in Norway, and the answer came back within seconds. "Kai Sorensen", I said at the same time as Beatrice said "Peter!"

"What", I asked.

"Peter Dalsrud", one of dad's mates. I can see him. He just got out of the car and is quarrelling with the police. But there are four cars in front of him. They are fucked. You have all the time in the world, Marius. Those guys are not going anywhere soon."

"YESSSS", I shouted back at her. "Right into the trap. I

can almost smell the gold, Beatrice, but don't go anywhere until they have been released and then let me know." I couldn't quite believe it, more than 30 kilos of gold was only minutes away. Too good to be true, but there and then I felt that this was the exception that proved the rule. I opened the boot, partly to show the driver where I was, but primarily to hide the registration plate which was at the bottom of the boot-lid of my Audi. The last few weeks I had let my beard grow. I was wearing a woollen beanie, and an over-sized fisherman's sweater. I could hardly recognise myself.

Just had to hope that nobody else would either.

~ ~ ~

Gunnar left. The situation was too chaotic to play cat and mouse with somebody who may not be there. Soon after he sat down in his office, Kai and Peter were second in the queue to get their fine, the taxi had just come out of the tunnel, with Joe only a few hundred metre behind. Kai had suggested that they should try to call the Taxi line and get the driver to pull over, since they had already concluded he couldn't be in on the deal, but they couldn't come up with a plausible explanation for such a request. The traffic was easing up as the ring-road widened to two lanes, and Peter could see on the tracking map that the taxi was gathering speed.

Four minutes later, Joe could get into the left lane and speed up, too. At the same time, Peter exclaimed, "he is not taking the exit to the car-park, he is continuing straight ahead."

"Shit. Are you sure", Gunnar said.

"If the tracking device is working, I am sure."

"Where should I go?" Joe asked.

"You'll just have to follow the taxi. Where is it now, Peter?"

"It took the next exit, it's going through the roundabout towards the entrance at the other side of the Shopping Centre.

Where are you Joe?"

"Getting close, just a few minutes behind, I'd say."

"Drive like a mad-man, Joe. In a few minutes the gold is getting away from us", Gunnar insisted, apoplectic at having been hoodwinked again.

~ ~ ~

At last I saw it coming, A-1208, as welcome as the sight of a lighthouse in a sea of fog. I got out of my car and waved at the driver. He flicked his high beam in response. He pulled up next to my car to align his boot with mine. "So you must be Sammy Davies, don't look much like him, though", he said with a smile.

"Yes, that's me, different fathers", I said, returning his smile. "Great that you got the message to come here instead. I am so pressed for time today. Can I ask you to give me a hand with the crates? I asked, "my back is out of kilter." I was trying not to move, in case he noticed my limp, and in case Gunnar would be questioning him later, very likely, I thought.

"No worries", he said and transferred both crates to the back of my car.

"What do I owe you?"

"The meter is on 1,420", he said in a somewhat opportunistic tone.

I counted out 2,000 kroner and gave it to him. "There you are, and keep the change. Great service, you saved me today."

He expressed his gratitude and drove away. In the back of my car was hopefully nine million in gold. Almost unreal. As I drove away, Nancy Sinatra started singing again.

"The boys have finally been let go. How is it going your end?"

"The crates are in the back of the car. I'll drive towards the Eastern Lake, check the content and get rid of the crates. Come to think of it, that's on the way to Sweden, so I might as well keep going?"

"So funny, Marius, very funny. Instead I suggest we meet at your place in about an hour. Just to be sure, take the outer ring-road on the way back. And Marius, you can look forward to monster sex tonight."

I laughed and hung up. Slapped my thighs a couple of times, to make sure I wasn't dreaming. Almost crashed into a car in front of me which had just pulled over and stopped. That would not have been good.

~ ~ ~

"The taxi is on the move again", Peter yelled, they had just rejoined traffic, a 4,200 kroner fine crumbled up between the seats. How far away are you, Joe?"

"Almost at the entrance to the shopping centre, less than a minute away, but what do I do? Follow the taxi or see if I can see why he stopped?"

"Get there and look for any signs of the crates", Gunnar commanded, "we can worry about the taxi later."

Joe tried to overtake, but there was too much traffic. "I'm approaching the roundabout at the main entrance", he said.

"The taxi should be coming in the other direction right now, you should see it", Peter said.

"I see it. I see it. It's coming towards me."

"Ignore it, keep driving towards the entrance, what can you see?" Gunnar was cajoling him.

Joe came around to the entrance, all he could see was a black station wagon signalling to pull out from the kerb. "I can see a car leaving. A black station wagon."

"Get the registration, Joe. Whatever you do, get the registration. Can you get a photo?" Gunnar persisted.

"No. Can't do that. I am almost past him. Registration no. is BR58193." And then, as he drove past, Joe got a clear view of the profile of the driver. He almost gagged as he recognised the man. From the front he wouldn't have, but side on he did, because he had been looking at the very same profile during

Gunnar' and Vivian's birthday party. And the reason he remembered was that it had reminded him of the cover of a Davy Crockett book he had read many times in his youth: The distinctive eyebrows, the proud curvature of the nose and the strongly chiselled chin.

"What's happening?" Gunnar shouted.

But Joe couldn't get a word out, he had passed the car which had now pulled out right behind him, and almost run into him as Joe stopped abruptly, then it drove past and kept going.

"Joe, what the fuck is happening? Joe!" Gunnar's voice was high pitched and panicky. He had stood up from his desk, banging both fists on the desk.

Joe sat quite still, his forehead pressed to the steering wheel, his eyes closed. Tears welling up. Again, Gunnar shouting in his ear. "What is happening Joe, for fucks sake, say something."

And then Peter came on the line: "I think I know what's happening." His voice hollow with resignation, the angry edge gone. I just got the reply to my registration plate inquiry. The owner of the car is Marius Tokle. Wasn't that the name of Beatrice's boyfriend?"

The Accident

Beatrice greeted me in a see-through negligee with a glass of champagne. I was carrying a large sports-bag over my left shoulder, containing more than 30 kilos of pure gold. It was hard to differentiate between the rush of our new-found riches or the relief of having avoided detection, or for that matter the excitement of seeing Beatrice dance half naked around the apartment. And the inevitable happened, of course. Within minutes of Beatrice checking that the coins were real, we were on her large, circular bed, not wearing much, and in classic Scrooge McDuck style we were bathing in gold coins. We poured them over each other, laughing and roaring at the ridiculousness of it. It all ended by her covering me from head to toe in gold coins, before riding me like a wild stallion into the sunset. It was by luck alone that I heard the alarm on my mobile go off on the way to the shower, reminding me that I had 15 minutes to delete the email before it would have been sent to The World newspaper and to the police.

~ ~ ~

After a fierce discussion on the phone, they agreed to meet back at Gunnar's home, as Vivian was away at the farm. Gunnar was so angry that he was wary of leaving the office, afraid that he might assault anyone he'd encounter on the way out. As he exited the car-park, he sideswiped a parked car, but he just continued at full speed. When Kai and Peter arrived at the door, he was already well into his third whisky. Five minutes later, Joe arrived, and they sat down in the lounge-room, all of them shaken up by the events of the afternoon in their own way.

"I knew it", Gunnar started intently, "deep down I had the feeling that whoever was writing those fucking emails was someone I knew, or at least someone who knew of me." He was cradling the glass so hard his knuckles were white, his hand shaking, threatening to spill the amber liquid.

"Do you remember I asked you", Peter continued, "why he was getting in touch now, three years later?"

"Yes, I do remember, kept me awake for several nights", Gunnar said and glared towards Kai. "If only Kai had told me that he had seen Beatrice and this Marius fellow in a black Audi Station Wagon the day after the party, I could have made the connection. Then all of this could have been avoided…"

"But how could I possibly know…?" Kai said, upset at being made a scapegoat.

"By using you head", Gunnar retorted, his voice shrill.

"Calm down, calm down", Peter interrupted, "let's not go there. It's not going to help the situation." After a lengthy pause, he said: "As a matter of fact, we were bloody lucky today. Our objective was to find out who was behind this, and we succeeded. If Joe had arrived only a few seconds later, we would have had nothing."

Peter cleared his throat a couple of times, before following up: "But the question we have to ask, Gunnar, whether you like it or not, is if Beatrice has anything to do with it?"

Following yet another long pause, Gunnar answered bitterly: "I have been considering it, but I just cannot make myself believe it." The answer was hanging in the air, but none of them dared to contradict him. It was Gunnar himself who went on: "One thing was the fighting during her teenage years, that happens in most families, but Beatrice is an adult now. And even if our relationship remains somewhat strained, she's still my daughter, my own flesh and blood. That she could have been part of it is just absurd."

"So what you believe", Peter maintained, "is that Marius somehow has used Beatrice to get close to you, in order to find out how much he could fleece you for?"

"Yes, that's the only way it makes any sense", Gunnar mumbled, swallowing his conclusion with a big mouthful of whisky.

Even though Peter didn't believe Gunnar's version, he just

didn't dare to confront him right now. And then neither did Kai nor Joe. Maybe reality would sink in during the next couple of days. For a change, it was Joe who broke the silence: "What are you going to do, Gunnar? How about we talk to him first? I had a long conversation with him at the party, he seemed quite nice."

"What did you say?" Gunnar stared at him. "He was nice?" Gunnar was spitting the words out: "Firstly, he insulted me at my own 50th birthday party. Secondly, he seduced my daughter so that he could extort us for all we are worth. I have never experienced anything more cynically manipulative. And you are telling me he is nice? That we should negotiate with him?"

"All I am saying is…"

"What Joe? That I should give this Marius fellow a call and tell him I know he's behind it, and that if he would be so kind as to return the gold, we'd be all square, everything forgotten. Is that what you are saying?"

"Well…"

"I'll tell you what will happen then, Joe. As soon as he finds out that I know who he is, he'll be calling the police. Then he'll want me locked up as soon as possible. And so will you in due course. Think about that, Joe."

"But Joe does have a point", Peter interjected, "for all we know he is not a career criminal. He runs a furniture import company. If he is arrested for blackmail, he'll lose the gold, the company and his freedom. that's not a bad start to negotiate from."

Gunnar looked like he had been hit in the face. "Have you lost your minds? You want to negotiate? Just because you have said hello to him once? Can't you see that he has treated us all like fools?"

Gunnar stood up and dragged Joe up from where he was sitting. "Get the fuck out of my house. You can go to hell, all of you!" Peter tried to hold Gunnar and calm him down, but all he got was an elbow in the midriff, making him double over. Joe had already escaped to the hallway. They would just have to grab their coats and get out before any serious harm was inflicted. They all knew that when Gunnar lost his temper like this, it was best just to get away. When outside, they all agreed to meet again in 24 hours to try to talk some sense into Gunnar.

~ ~ ~

The next day, I managed to get up around lunchtime. I dropped by home on the way to work and 'hid' my Monster Box at the bottom of my wardrobe, threw a towel over it, promising myself to organise a bank deposit box ASAP. I put a gold coin in my pocket, wanting to give Brad a reward for his assistance. 9,000 for an hour's work was pretty well paid, even Brad would agree. And even if I was now a man of means, the gold was for holidays and for my pension. Work was still work, and there would be emails and paperwork piled up over the past week. In addition, we were preparing for a furniture fair, the next few days would be busy.

It was evening and dark by the time I turned the lights off and left the office. Beatrice was out on the town with a girlfriend, so I had planned to go visit Brad on the boat and give him his coin, maybe score supper. Just as I passed the garbage container at the back of the office building on my way to the car-park, I heard a sound behind me. Then I didn't hear anything else for a while.

I woke up with intense pain in my neck and shoulder, crouched on my side in the foetal position in a dark space, which I soon realised was the boot of a car. My mouth was stuffed with what felt like a sock, kept in place by gaffer tape, also used around my hands and feet, my torso and knees tucked into my chest. Every time the car hit a bump in the road, it felt like my shoulder was given an electric shock. Even in the haze of pain, I knew who was driving. I soon also realised where we were heading, as I was constantly pressed back onto what I assumed was the bottom of the boot-lid as the car ascended towards the cottage. And I thought this was not going to end well.

The car stopped. The boot opened and I was blinded by a torch light, lifted up and rolled out, hitting the ground head first. Then I was rolled along the ground like a barrel of barley, until I could feel a threshold underneath and found myself in what turned out to be a woodshed. Once inside, he cut the tape so I could gingerly stretch out my body. He said nothing, but I could sense his smirk of malevolence, enjoying my misery. I was lying on the ground, body straightened, but still with tape around my feet and hands, the only sound was my whimpering and the rustle of a tarpaulin underneath me.

"You will die tonight", was the first thing he said. He might as well have told me what was for dinner. I was rather preoccupied trying to contain the pain and gather my wits, not being able to worry about what would happen later. All I could see through the tears was the glare of a torch which came from a headlamp, and the steam from his breath, like a one eyed troll. Something hit my bad knee. I curled up, made myself small, tried to disappear. The troll just sat there, breathing, waiting.

"Where is the gold?" he said next. The gold. It was hard to think, as if my nervous system had been shattered and shut down half my brain. How did Gunnar know about the gold? Had he managed to track me down? Had Beatrice betrayed me? Or was it a bluff? What did I have to lose? I was going to die anyway. "What gold?" I whispered through cracked lips.

"This", he said, flicking something towards me. I got a glimpse of a shadow in the light and realised that it was the coin I had meant to give to Brad. Again, what did I have to lose, so I pretended we were equals, seated around the negotiating table, clearing up a small misunderstanding. "Ah, that gold", I said as audaciously as my general state would allow.

Gunnar came towards me, put a boot in my abdomen, a rifle against my throat. His voice full of pent-up anger: "If all you had done was to abuse my family and steal a lot of money from me, I would still have killed you, Marius, but maybe not without scruples." He paused for effect. "But because you are also a smug, arrogant shithead from the snobby part of town, it won't cost me more grief than the effort it takes to pull the trigger." He pushed down, I gagged, leading to convulsions raking my ravaged body. He backed off, gave me some room to suffer. When I had almost stopped shaking, he said: "I'll ask you one last time, Marius. Where is the gold?"

I didn't have a strategy, no longer capable of coherent thought, not even trying to be clever. "One box is at my place … the other with Beatrice", I stammered through tears and bile, defeated.

Gunnar bent over me like a grizzly bear, hit me across the head several times, before dragging me up into a sitting position and with the unmistakable smell of alcohol on his breath shouted right in my face: "No fucking way! Beatrice is not part of this!"

I felt like I was about to faint, but managed to stutter: "Yes, she is … she … she was standing on the pedestrian bridge close to where Peter was pulled over by the police."

Gunnar let go, kept standing over me before backing up, turned around and left. I could hear a latch falling into place. With what little strength I had left, I called after him: "If you kill me, you'll have to kill Beatrice, too."

Gunnar had to think. He wandered around in circles outside, angrily kicking at roots and pebbles on the ground. Was it true? How would Marius have known that Peter and Kai had been pulled over if he didn't have an accomplice? And this person could have been anybody. But they had been in Kai's car, and Marius had said it was Peter who he had seen talking to the police. And if so, Marius must have had someone there who recognised Peter. Could it still be Joe? He and Marius had obviously gotten to know each other at the party. No, it couldn't have been Joe, he was the one who had given them Marius' registration number. If they had been in cahoots, Joe wouldn't have done that.

Gunnar stopped, his hands clammy as he felt a wave of anxiety roll over him, literally making his head feel burning hot. It could not be denied. Beatrice had betrayed him. His own flesh and blood. What was he going to do? If Marius disappeared, Beatrice would understand what had happened. And she would not remain silent. If she had betrayed him once, she'd do it again. He would have to talk to her, get her to see the big picture. This Marius fellow on one side, and then her family, uncles Joe, Kai and Peter on the other. And the gold.

He felt deflated and miserable as he went into the cabin and made a cup of coffee, added some whisky. He had destroyed Marius' mobile and thrown the pieces in a garbage container, so he would have to use his own. It was past midnight. No answer on the first attempt, nor the second. The third time she answered: "Yes, what is it?" she said flatly.

"Gold", Gunnar said. He had thought that if she knew nothing after all, she'd just hang up, or accuse him of being drunk or crazy. But if she hesitated, or started asking what he was on about, then he'd know that she was involved one way or another. When the reaction came after a few seconds, it was clear enough: "fuck."

Gunnar felt an irresistible urge to scream, but couldn't get a word out. He slouched down in a chair, looked incomprehensibly at a photo of Beatrice on the mantel piece. Feebly he asked: "But why, Beatrice? Why?"

"Why?, she screamed back at him. "I'll ask you why, dad. Why did you kill Steve?"

"Because…"

"Exactly, dad. Because, because … You are a murderer. You even killed a friend. For money. So don't you accuse me of anything."

Gunnar was about to explain, desperately wanted her to understand, but was stuck for words. Before he could compose himself, she went on: "But how …" Then she screamed: "Marius, where is Marius?"

Gunnar could sense he was about to lose his grip. He knew his daughter as well as he knew himself. Neither of them would cower to the whip, but could be persuaded, especially if the carrot was big enough. If he was going to steer this boat to safety, he would have to offer her something bigger than Marius. He thought he knew what that was: "I've got him here. At the cabin. He is doing OK."

"Damned it dad, did you hurt him? I'll go straight to the police. Let me speak to him. NOW!"

"Calm down, Beatrice, you will speak to him. But first I you and I need to talk." Beatrice tried to interrupt, but Gunnar pressed on: "I don't care what you have done, Beatrice. I forgive you. I want you to keep the gold. Including Marius' share, call it an advance on your inheritance. Nine million, Beatrice, a small fortune."

There was a short pause, just long enough for Gunnar to start believing that he had succeeded. But when the response came, it was with utter contempt in her voice: "Do you really believe you can buy me, dad? Do you actually believe that? That would have made me no better than you. I'll prove you wrong. If I don't get to speak to Marius within one minute, I'll hang up and call the police."

"But Beatrice, think about it. You'll tire of Marius, just like you have all your other boyfriends, and then …"

She interrupted: "Didn't you hear me, dad? NO. NO. NO. The clock is ticking. In 50 seconds I'll hang up."

"But my dear girl, we are family. We may have had disagreements on this and that, but in a storm, we stick together. Are you choosing a criminal in favour of your own family?"

"38, 37, 36."

Gunnar stood up and walked towards the door. "Beatrice, for god's sake, think about it. You'll get nine million to turn your back. It will soon be over between you and Marius, we both know that. You'll regret this, Beatrice. Think, nine million."

"18, 17, 16."

"OK, OK, Beatrice, you can speak to him", Gunnar said with resignation as he opened the door to the woodshed. He kicked Marius lightly, curled up in the corner. Marius stirred, moaning, disoriented. "Here he is", Gunnar lent down, put the phone to Marius' ear.

"Marius, are you there?" Beatrice asked.

"Hmmm … what?"

"Marius, are you OK?"

"Beatrice … I … I am cold …"

"DAD", Beatrice shouted, loud enough for Gunnar to hear it.

"I had to get him to come with me", Gunnar started, but she stopped him short.

"Fuck you, dad. What have you done to him?"

"I hit him in the head with a baseball bat. I didn't have a choice. But it's not too serious."

"Listen, dad!" Beatrice said, her voice sharp, "I am getting in the car. He says he's cold, so you give him a blanket. I am sure you'll find some pain-killers in the medicine cabinet. Give him four. If you kill him, dad, you'll have to kill me, too. So think carefully about how you'll explain that your daughter has disappeared, as has her boyfriend, that you have just bought nine million worth of gold, and that the disappearance of your friend Steve remains a mystery after three years. In addition, you have just used your mobile at the cabin, so they'll know where to start looking." Then she hung up.

Gunnar did as he was told, realised he had to keep Marius alive for now. Then he sat down back inside the cabin, bewildered. Right now it was looking like Beatrice would take Marius with her. Could he live with that? Knowing that they could give him up to the police at any time? What would happen when they ran out of gold? Would they demand more? It would be like sitting on death row not knowing when the executioner was arriving. He would be totally dependent on two people, in his estimation two rather volatile people, who on a bad day could take it out on him. That didn't feel like something he could live with. But what was the alternative? He knew he could kill Marius and bury him under the rocks next to Steve. But he couldn't kill Beatrice. And, hypothetically, if that was the only option, what then of Vivian?

When Gunnar saw the headlights of a car approaching the cabin he had been through every scenario, from eradicating his whole family to letting Beatrice take Marius home without any conditions attached, but he still didn't have a clear plan. He grabbed the rifle and walked outside. What he saw, was alarming. The car was not Beatrice's Mini, but Vivian's Mercedes. And when mother and daughter alighted from each side of the car, he realised that his options had narrowed considerably.

"I brought mum", Beatrice said, "just to be safe. Where is Marius?" Gunnar pointed to the woodshed.

"What are you doing here, Vivian? You don't need to get involved in this", Gunnar said trying to grab her with his unoccupied hand.

"When my daughter has become involved in this devilish calamity, I have no choice. I no longer know what you are capable of", she said, wresting free from his grip, "and put down the gun, before we have any more accidents out here."

"My God", they could hear despairingly from the woodshed, "you have almost killed him. Mum, come here, I need help." The two of them managed to get Marius up in a sitting position, removing the tape from around his arms and legs. "And you, get a glass of water and a warm cloth. And another blanket", she barked at Gunnar, who had no choice but to obey. He put the rifle up against the wall behind the woodshed door.

It took a few minutes to wake Marius from his daze. His neck and shoulder was still throbbing, but the pain-killers had dulled the worst of the pain. Beatrice was on her knees next to him, Vivian sat on the chopping block.

"What do we do now?", Gunnar said from the open door.

"We are taking Marius to the emergency ward. Then we'll see", Beatrice answered.

"I can't let you take him with you unless we have some sort of agreement. Don't you understand that he'll ruin our lives."

"And how is that going to work? I suppose we can agree on anything here and now, and then we'll renege as soon as we get into town. How naive can you be?" Beatrice said.

"So you mean you'll keep half the gold, Marius the other half, and then you'll keep your mouths shut for all eternity? That's a situation I just can't live with, it's as simple as that", Gunnar said firmly.

"If you leave us alone, we'll leave you alone. After today, we'll never need to meet again", Beatrice said, nailing Gunnar with her eyes.

But Gunnar stood firm, positioned himself right in the middle of the door opening, hands on hips, immovable. "Nobody gets out of here until we have an agreement."

"Don't you understand anything, dad?" Beatrice whined. "An agreement is worthless. There is no trust between us. You either have to kill us, or let us go."

The last sentence hung silently in the air. Minutes went by. Nobody moved, nobody said a word. Finally, Beatrice stood up and walked towards Gunnar. Vivian wedged herself between them. "Let us out, dad. We have to get Marius to the hospital.

He is not looking well." Gunnar pushed them both backwards, Beatrice almost tripping over Marius.

"I don't give a shit if we stay here all night. And all day tomorrow. Nobody is leaving until we have agreed what happens from here." Again, Beatrice was about to object, but Vivian interrupted her: "There is a way we can resolve this, but it will hurt, especially for the two of you", she said looking at Beatrice and Marius, who were now seated on the ground next to each other. "But you deserve it in a way, there are no angels left here anymore."

"What do you mean, mum? What are you thinking?" Beatrice looked at her mother with alarm.

"I have to break our agreement, Beatrice. I'm sorry. But you have brought this on yourself. So you'll have to suffer the consequences." Beatrice stared at her mother for a few seconds, her eyes wide open, then comprehension rolled over her like an avalanche.

"No mum, no, no, not that … that's not necessary." Beatrice reached a hand out to Vivian who took it in both of hers.

"Yes, Beatrice, I'm afraid it is. It's the only way out of this ungodly mess, so that's the way it's got to be." Vivian lent forward and kissed her daughter on the forehead, before turning to Gunnar.

"We'll give you our guarantees, Gunnar, and then you'll let us go."

Gunnar looked inquisitively at his wife of 30 years. The last few years had taken a particularly hard toll on the marriage, but he still loved her. He had held quite a few things from her over the years, mostly to protect her, but now it seemed like she and Beatrice had secrets, too. "Let me hear it", he said, with poorly concealed scepticism.

"The situation", she began, turning back towards Beatrice and Marius, "is that you both know that Gunnar killed Steve." They both nodded hesitantly. "What you have to do, is to give

Gunnar something in return." Marius looked questioningly at Beatrice, who in turn glared hard at her mother.

But Vivian didn't waver. "Listen, you did something incredibly stupid extorting money from Gunnar. And now you have been caught. it's going to cost you, one way or another. Either you own up, or I'll dob you in."

Marius was preoccupied with his pain, but nodded vaguely. Beatrice had shrivelled up, looked pathetic as she lent against Marius in the corner. In the end she nodded, too.

"OK", Vivian said, more than uncomfortable with what she was about to say. "I'll start with you, Marius, as it really is all about you. Beatrice has told me, in full confidence, that it was you who swapped the by now infamous manhole cover, leading to the sudden demise of a certain pizza restaurant owner, breaking his leg, and then he had a stroke. Is that right, Marius?"

"Yeah."

"Is that all?" Gunnar said sarcastically, "a practical joke that went awry?"

"No, that's not all", Vivian said, "because that guy is one of the most feared stand over men in Oslo's underworld. If he gets wind that Marius did it … well, you can figure it out."

"OK, I'll buy that", Gunnar said with a scornful smirk.

"And what about Beatrice?" Gunnar asked, with curiosity, "I don't dare to think about what shit she's been up to that I don't already know about?"

"Are you sure you want to know, Gunnar? Is it not enough that you have it over Marius?" Vivian asked with anxious sincerity.

"Hey, she said it herself, we can no longer trust each other", Gunnar said, without mercy.

Vivian drew her breath a couple of times and said: "Twelve years ago, when Beatrice was 15, she stole a car when drunk. She had met a bloke she liked. Wanted to go visit him in the middle of the night. On her way there, she careened into the oncoming traffic, sliding into the side of another car which lost control, drove off the road and hit a tree. Everyone in the car was killed. All three of them."

"Yes, I remember that, not far from here", Gunnar said, stunned. "They were looking for a blue car, a Ford I think, but they never found it?"

"That's right", Vivian said, "they never found it."

Gunnar stared at Beatrice, then back to Vivian, unsure of what to say, when the silence was broken by a deep, guttural wail from the depths of hell. It was Marius.

Love Hurts

After being brought to the emergency ward in the centre of Oslo, I was transferred to another hospital, where I had surgery on my shoulder the next day. It was the same deal as the knee, more wires and pins. When I came to from the anaesthetic, Vivian was sitting by the bed, holding my hand. The tears flowing. And she barely left my side for the next few days. The police paid me a visit, routine for anyone brought in with an unidentified impact injury, I guess. All I told them was that I had been assaulted on the street. Gratuitous violence not unusual on the streets of Oslo. They were far from convinced, but what could they do? Vivian was in control. Beatrice had temporarily not been allowed to visit, but Brad did a couple of times.

When the worst of the pain had subsided, and I was feeling sort of level-headed again, Vivian told me everything about what had happened twelve years earlier. Beatrice had called in the middle of night, crying uncontrollably. In the end she had managed to explain that she had stolen a car and thought she might have caused an accident. She didn't quite know. She had then driven to the cabin more or less on auto-pilot. Vivian told her to stay put, and that she'd come and get her straight away. On the way there, she heard about a fatal accident on local radio.

When she arrived at the cabin, she found a blue Ford with dents along one side and a broken rear light. Beatrice had collapsed on the couch inside. On the early morning news she heard that three people had died in one car, a man and a woman and their 13-year-old daughter. police were looking for another car, believed to have been involved, a dark blue Ford sedan.

Vivian took full responsibility for what had happened afterwards. Beatrice was in a state of shock, unable to do anything, just lying on the couch, shivering. And Vivian could not make herself report her daughter to the police, facing a triple charge of manslaughter, even if she'd be tried as a minor. She just couldn't do it. So they stayed at the cabin all of the next day. The following night, Vivian drove the Ford on remote forest roads until she got to a spot by a deep pond where she was able to push the car in, never to be found. She walked for three hours through the woods back to the cabin.

When they were back home, reading the papers and learning that the deceased 13-year-old had a brother of 17 who had not been in the car at the time, it made it all so much worse. Until then, they were comforted knowing that since the whole family had died, there was a kind of finality to it. A terrible tragedy, but nobody left bereaved. A dark blue Ford had been reported stolen earlier the night of the accident, but it had never been found. The accident was irreversible. There were no witnesses. The car was 20 metre under the surface of a remote pond. Vivian and Beatrice had been in a daze, unable to sleep for a week, when one morning they decided to try to claw back their lives.

What did I feel? Most of all I felt shame for not feeling much at all. It was such a long time ago now. I didn't remember much from the aftermath of the accident, as if I had been blindly walking through a storm. When the storm was over, I never looked back. There was most likely an undetonated grenade somewhere deep in my subconscious, but I had never tried to locate it. And I had no desire to find it now.

After a week, when Vivian concluded I had regained enough of my senses, she allowed Beatrice to visit me. The killer of my father, my mother and my sister. But the overarching feeling I had was that of gratitude that she still wanted me. How could I blame her for what had happened?

She was 15 and drunk. I, too, had been 15 and drunk. Even if I hadn't stolen cars myself, I had been a passenger in one more than once. The difference was luck. And I still drove under the influence, even if I claimed to be in complete control. Moreover, I was in no doubt that Vivian and Beatrice had saved my life in the woodshed. Mother and daughter having both exposed themselves to get me out of there alive. So for what it was worth, I forgave her. She cried and told me she loved me.

When we had finished with the tears and the hugs and the kisses, there was still a question I needed answered: Did she know who I was that evening at the reunion party, and did I seduce her, or was it the other way around? She laughed at first, told me she had known who I was all along, but she didn't want to have any contact. She said she had been desperate to know how I was coping, and made discreet enquiries about me, but considered it an impossibility to have anything to do with me. So every time we'd meet in passing or at some function, she'd put on her arrogant demeanour, which she knew deterred even the most persistent of suitors. But when she had seen me with a limp and a cane at the reunion and noticed I was staring at her, she had thrown caution to the wind and returned my smile. Twice. Curiosity, assisted by the alcohol, had taken over. So when it came to who had seduced whom on the night, it was difficult to say. We both had ulterior motives. We both should have turned away. We both chose the opposite.

A Quandary

Gunnar was furious. Vivian was by Marius' bedside almost round-the-clock. He couldn't believe it. In addition, she had acquired a worryingly persistent determination that he hadn't seen from her for many years. She had even stopped drinking. And every time he tried to explain to her what a vulnerable position they were in, she was steadfast in her rejection. If that wasn't enough, he had found out that his daughter had been responsible for a car accident, amounting to manslaughter, abetted by her mother, and they had kept it a secret from him. The ones close to him were not to be trusted. On the other hand, they could no longer pester him for the murder of Steve. They were guilty of taking lives, too. The only obstacle left was Marius.

~ ~ ~

The doorbell chimed. Beatrice was not expecting visitors and was also not in the mood for company, so she remained on her couch, reading a magazine. But when the chiming persisted for several minutes, she stood up and spoke into the intercom, "Yes, who is it?"

"It's dad. Let me in, Beatrice. We have to talk."

Beatrice froze, felt her body tense up just from hearing his voice, sensed the veiled threat between the simple words, something only she and Vivian could pick up on. "No", she said coldly and hung up, but remained by the door, listening. She heard the click of the front door, and then footsteps coming up the stairs.

There was a knock on the door. Beatrice retreated slowly backwards.

"Let me in, Beatrice. I only want to have a chat", Gunnar tried again, this time sounding as if he was offended. As

Beatrice sat back down, she heard the lock turning, and the entrance door opening.

"What the hell?" Beatrice yelled, "you haven't got a key to my apartment. And mum would not have given it to you voluntarily. So you have fuckin' nicked it from her keyring."

"Relax, Beatrice, calm down. I just want to talk. Just listen to what I have to say, and then I'll leave. That can't be so bad", he said and sat down in one of the designer chairs.

Beatrice stood up, she would rather stand than sit, crossed her arms in defiance, leaning against the frame of the door to the kitchen. "OK, out with it, if it's so damned important."

Gunnar was sitting upright with his feet apart, leaning forward, elbows on his knees, hands flat together. "Yes, I am sorry I hit Marius as hard as I did. It wasn't my intention to hurt him that much."

"No", Beatrice scowled, "the intention was to kill him, right. Find out where the gold was, shoot him and then dump him next to Steve. Don't come here telling me you were going to let him go afterwards. I don't buy it."

"But don't you get it, Beatrice. On one hand is what he could do to me. But now the situation is much worse. You eradicated his whole family. Do you really think he'll forgive you for that?" Gunnar paused, letting it sink in. Beatrice didn't bat an eyelid, looked down on the floor, balancing one shoe on her toes, disinterested.

Gunnar went on: "Well, maybe he'll leave it for now. While he is in need of tender loving care. Feeling vulnerable. But what about in two or three months time, Beatrice? When everything goes back to normal. Meat and potatoes in brown gravy. Do you reckon he will still feel that it was OK that you killed his family?" Gunnar opened his hands in front of him, tried to tease out some reaction from Beatrice, but she hadn't moved, displaying no reaction, still staring at the floor. He wanted to throw her across his lap and give her a thorough thrashing to beat some sense into her, just like the old days, but he realised those days were gone. If he was going to get anywhere with her, he had to curb his anger, so he continued in the same conciliatory tone: "Look at what he did with the pizza guy. He didn't rush things. But over time he couldn't live with what he had endured. And in the end he got his revenge, despite the risk. Ingenuous, too. Very impressive. But I have to ask myself: why will he let you and mum go unpunished, when what you did to him was so much more grievous?"

Gunnar leaned back in the chair, quite pleased with himself. He had managed to say what he had come for. Beatrice was a smart girl. She would understand. Maybe not today, maybe not for a few days, but in a few weeks, then she'd see the light...

Beatrice lifted her head and looked at Gunnar, feigning indifference. "Was that all? Then you can go", she said, pointing towards the door.

Gunnar shook his head in exasperation. "But are you totally blind, my girl? Can't you see that with one phone call he can get us all behind bars. He has all the power, and he will use it. Believe me."

"Indeed, what can I believe", Beatrice said icily, "that you promised to leave when you had said your piece? Go dad, go! I don't want you here. And I am not your 'girl' any more, so stop calling me that."

Gunnar stood up abruptly and walked towards the door. On his way out he turned around and pointed his index finger at Beatrice: "Call me when you understand. I'll take care of the rest", he said and left.

~ ~ ~

When I was discharged from hospital a couple of weeks later, Beatrice took over from her mum. She attended to my every need as if she had never done anything else. When Beatrice had to go to London for a few days, Vivian stood in for her. So, the practicalities of life were not an issue. But what did I really feel about Beatrice and me? Was her excessive care an expression of true love, pity, a bad conscience or at worst a calculated ploy to make me feel trusting and amiable? I hoped intensely it was the former, but couldn't quite let go of the thought that it was the latter. As for me, I meant what I said, that I forgave them both for what had happened. It was an accident. Accidents happen. Even if Beatrice and Vivian were punished, I'd never get my family back. A bit like being able to live with Beatrice being a high-class prostitute in London. Pragmatist to a fault. So be it. It worked for me.

~ ~ ~

Then one evening, when Beatrice had stopped by her own apartment, she found Gunnar sitting on her couch. He admitted to having copied her keys. "What I am about to tell you, Beatrice, is much more important than the copying of keys", he said dismissively.

"I don't want to know!" Beatrice shouted at him. "Get out."

Gunnar grabbed her and pushed her down on the couch next to him. "You are going to listen to this, Beatrice. Aron is dying. Do you understand what that means? That Marius is off the hook. We've got nothing on him anymore. He'll be able to do whatever he wants."

Beatrice hesitated, before asking, her voice thick with scepticism: "How do you know?"

Gunnar released his grip on her wrist. "I got in touch with a nurse I know at the convalescent home where Aron was being treated. She told me that Aron Tollefsen had another stroke and is now in intensive care at Oslo Hospital. When I called there, they asked me if I was family, because nobody else was allowed to visit, as he is definitely nearing the end. Meaning that everyone had left him. Probably because he no longer posed a threat to anyone. So even if we leaked to Aron's underworld buddies that we know who was behind the fake manhole cover, nobody would care any more." Gunnar could tell that Beatrice was not unmoved by what he had said, her brows narrowing.

"That doesn't change anything", Beatrice said. "We love each other, we trust each other, and we'll get through this together. Now I want you to go", she said and stood up.

"Well, think about it. In a few days or weeks at the most, you'll read in the paper that Aron Tollefsen is dead. The journalists will dig up the story about the wooden manhole cover again, which Marius will be sure to read, too. Then we'll see how strong the love is", he said and left her standing there. Beatrice sat back down, thinking. Then she googled a locksmith.

~ ~ ~

Over the next few weeks, Beatrice couldn't help thinking about what her dad had said. She was especially worried about what would happen when Aron Tollefsen did die, Gunnar had a point there, and what if she and Marius did split up? Deep down she knew that neither of them were the marrying kind, and that the day would come when the passion would wane. How would Marius handle that? Would the past come back and haunt him, with dire consequences for both of them, and if so, also for her mother? The distance between love and hate can be very short. She needed to speak to her mum about it some more.

As for Gunnar, he was biding his time, with great difficulty, hoping that Beatrice would eventually see things his way, yet deep down doubting it would happen. Hence, he was in a foul mood most of the time, snapping at people at work, to the extent that they avoided him as best as they could. Not all that difficult, Gunnar spent most days brooding in his office with the door closed. At home, he and Vivian didn't see much of each other, either, and when they did, not much was said. A couple of times he tried to talk to her about the threat posed to them all, but especially to Beatrice. "You know as well as I do, that the relationship between them won't last, what then, how do you think Marius will react?" Gunnar said, without getting any reaction from Vivian. But the second time, pointing out the significance of Aron dying to her, she did at least answer, "well that changes things, doesn't it?" said with scorn as she turned her back at him, walking away to end the conversation. Gunnar still thought that maybe, just maybe, Vivian would eventually come around to his point-of-view.

Three weeks after they had last met at her apartment, Aron Tollefsen died. The day after, Beatrice rang Gunnar. "Hi dad. I'm sorry. I have had several sleepless nights, and I think I get what you mean. Sensing something with Marius, too. He is not the same, avoids meeting my eyes. The other day I overheard him discussing something on the phone in hushed tones with his best mate, Brad. I got up while he was sleeping the following night and checked the recent search history on his PC. 'poison' and 'poisoning' came up quite a bit. So as difficult as this is to admit, I think you are right. Sooner or later he'll take his revenge. I am scared."

Gunnar felt a huge relief. At long last she had come to her senses, the family was back together again. "You have no idea how happy I am that you rang, Beatrice. This is something we can still fix, but we have to act now."

"I don't like it, dad. I don't want to know the details." She was on the verge of crying, had trouble finishing the sentence.

"Don't worry, Beatrice. I'll take care of it. Maybe you should go to London for a few days. Best if you are not around."

"Yes, that sounds like a good idea."

"You do that, Beatrice, it'll sort itself out", Gunnar assured her.

"Or maybe…"

"Maybe what, Beatrice?"

Beatrice composed herself as she said: "I had a thought. Marius and I have talked about spending a few days at the cabin, now that he is feeling better. I would cook dinner, we'd curl up in front of the fireplace, drink red wine and have a romantic time. He thought it sounded like a great idea, to get away for a while."

"Do you mean that, Beatrice, that you can organise that?"

"Yes, pretty sure I can. And I am the one who has messed this up, so I feel I need to contribute a bit, if I can… I reckon I can also lose his mobile before we leave, hide it in his apartment. He is always disorganised, so it won't be unusual."

"How about Thursday afternoon? That would work perfectly", Gunnar said with a hopeful voice.

"I think that'll work."

"I'll be there around 6pm, pretend that I am just coming by to check that everything is in order. And then you can sneak out, drive away, and I'll take care of the rest."

"It makes me sick to think about it, dad, but I do understand that it has to be done. Sooner or later he'll turn against me. Then it's him against us, him against the family. You were right all along, dad."

The Reckoning

Gunnar felt an unusual sense of calm driving towards the cabin that day. Even Vivian had finally come to her senses, having admitted that she, too, was afraid of what could happen to Beatrice. Ironic that they had to go through all this drama before they could unite as a family again. When this was over, he would do everything he could to maintain the peace and harmony. He would try to accept that Beatrice was a high-class prostitute. Not that he didn't have his own history of transgressions in that department. And he'd have to not be so hard on Vivian, let her get on with her life, without him having to be in control of everything.

Although he could feel the tension building up in his body, he realised he was looking forward to it more than dreading what he was about to do. Marius Tokle had hoodwinked him twice, fleeced him for more than ten million, and even involved his own daughter in the damned racket. And he was now more of a threat than ever to his whole family, so Gunnar had no scruples. Deep down he was looking forward to the moment when Marius would realise that Beatrice had stabbed him in the back. The ultimate betrayal. The act of firing the gun didn't bother him much. It was just something that had to be done. He also relished the thought of burying Marius under the rocks next to Steve. They sort of belonged together - without Steve, no Marius. He had left his mobile at home, and the rifle was locked up at the cabin. He was about to end the nightmare.

When he arrived in front of the cabin and got out, there was a car there, but not one that he recognised. Maybe a rent-a-car Marius had? Maybe he needed to drive an automatic because of the shoulder injury? He would have to investigate further. Either way, he was just passing by. Marius, limping, his arm still in a sling, posed no danger to him.

Gunnar was halfway to the front door when it swung open. Vivian stepped out, holding the rifle. Gunnar stopped in his stride, as if he had seen the devil incarnate himself. They stood there glaring at each other until Gunnar snapped out of his momentary stupor and said with obvious bewilderment: "What the hell are you doing here?"

Vivian didn't move, holding the rifle steadily in front of her, but not quite able to hide the fear in her voice: "You came here to kill Marius, Gunnar. Just as easy as you killed Steve. You just won't give up. You cannot stop." Pausing for breath, she went on: "Marius has a friend who knows the whole story. Are you going to kill him, too?" Vivian took a couple of steps towards Gunnar who backed off. "The only real threat is you, Gunnar. You and your delusions, your ghosts." Vivian took another couple of steps forward, and Gunnar retreated further. "Beatrice and I did something unforgivable to Marius twelve years ago. Nobody is to touch that boy. Especially not you. You are the one putting us all at peril." Vivian stopped, planted her feet wider apart, before she said: "Do you know where you are standing right now, Gunnar? On the very same spot Steve was standing when you shot him."

Gunnar looked around. Yes, she was right, he was standing on the same, large rock close to the water. But this was ridiculous. Vivian didn't have it in her. She was just trying to scare him. He would have to talk some sense into her. "Seriously, Vivian, give me the rifle", he said, stretching out his hand.

Vivian fired. The sound of the shot reverberated across the water. But there was nobody on the island that evening.

Epilogue

Gunnar was reported missing Saturday evening, following his non-attendance at a business meeting on Friday, and his mobile phone was found at his home. The same day we had sent an anonymous letter to the police that simply read: "Steve Hall, Aron Tollefsen, Gunnar Fergusen, Factory Outlet Stores." The addition of Aron Tollefsen was something Vivian, Beatrice and I had discussed at length when we planned how to kill Gunnar, and make sure we'd get away with it. We figured that the police would soon make the connection between Gunnar and Steve, and establish the motivation. Throwing Aron into the mix, a known criminal and likely killer would lead them on a wild goose chase. Eventually, we hoped, leading to conclusions of his involvement that couldn't be proven, but didn't need to be either, Aron was dead, too, after all.

Killing Gunnar had been Vivian's idea in the first place; I think she had come to the realisation that she would never be free of him, and she felt that she owed me, despite my protestations. Beatrice admitted to being torn between her love for me and her fear of what the future might hold, but in the end her mother convinced her that Gunnar would never change his ways, and would forever remain a threat to all of them.

Vivian also knew, of course, that she would be a prime suspect, and both Vivian and Beatrice were interviewed by the police the following week, me the week after to corroborate their alibi. Gunnar's time of disappearance was established as Thursday evening according to the mobile phone logs, an evening where Vivian, Beatrice and I allegedly had dinner together at Beatrice's apartment. Which is where our mobile logs said we had been. Our alibis were solid. The truth was that both Vivian and Beatrice had been at the cabin on the

Thursday, driving there in a borrowed car. Vivian had wanted to get Gunnar alone, Beatrice had been inside the cabin when it happened. But they had to move the body together, and get rid of Gunnar's car, not returning to Beatrice's apartment until 2am. They were both rather traumatised by it all, and I was worried about how they would handle the coming weeks; needlessly so, as it turned out.

Vivian's first police interview was mainly about her and Gunnar, and about the marriage. She told them the truth, that it had been difficult, especially the last few years. That they had often lived apart, that they had talked about divorce. Yes, he had at times seemed depressed, but she didn't believe he was suicidal. Yes, they owned a luxury unit in Oslo West, another apartment, the cabin by the lake, and a boat moored at a marina south of Oslo. No, she had no idea of what had happened.

In the second interview they brought up the disappearance of Steve Hall, and Gunnar's role in the Factory Outlet Store. Yes, she had known Steve Hall well and was still wondering what had happened to him. And when she was asked if she thought that Gunnar could have had anything to do with his disappearance, she said straight out 'no'. Even when they outlined the connection between Steve, the centre development and Gunnar, she stood by her husband. Why were they digging this up now? Should they not focus on what had happened to Gunnar?

During a third interview, they asked Vivian if she knew Aron Tollefsen. Vivian acknowledged she had heard the name, but couldn't recollect if it was in connection with Gunnar or not.

Then it went quiet. The police visited the farm, the cabin and the boat, without uncovering anything of interest. But one day the police were at the door and wanted to see some gold that Gunnar had bought earlier that autumn. We had prepared for that, and both the Monster Boxes were in the safe. So except for bewilderment, and, according to Vivian, a look of considerable envy from the police officers, that gave them nothing to go on, either.

After about a week, the media picked up on the eventuality that Gunnar's disappearance could have something to do with the disappearance of Steve Hall, three years earlier, and the circus was in full swing. Within 24 hours, the connection between Steve Hall, Factory Outlet Stores and Gunnar had been made, and Gunnar was variously referred to as "businessman and property developer" and "alleged killer", until one newspaper couldn't help it and plastered his name on the front page. The photo of the "class of 1982", where killer and victim stood a metre apart, as well as the 2007 reenactment, both became public sensations. But the killer had disappeared as mysteriously as the victim. Who had killed the killer? Or were the police barking up the wrong tree?

Then, after another week or so, Aron Tollefsen came to light, in words and pictures, as the one who allegedly had killed Steve Hall, contracted to do so by Gunnar Fergusen. Everything was falling into place as we had planned.

The police, unable to find hard evidence, had been leaking tidbits to the press, who had started digging further, and tracked down a nurse at the convalescent centre where Aron had been treated. She had divulged that Gunnar had been there, asking about Aron, a few weeks before Aron died. The day after, another nurse, this time from the Oslo Hospital could reveal a similar query on the phone. The mobile phone log later confirmed that the call had been made by Gunnar. The connection between them now firmly established, even though it had never existed. That evening we popped the champagne. It started to look like Vivian would survive further scrutiny.

What didn't survive, was the relationship between Beatrice

and I. As long as we were running around extorting people or planning a murder, the adrenalin was flowing, and every day was like a new episode of CSI. But neither of us were comfortable in an everyday routine, nor would we ever be. The day we started eating frozen meals at home it was all over. We both understood it. What surprised me was that I handled it well. Everything in life has a saturation point, beauty too, and I had my fill. In the long run she was too much for me, and in a way it was a relief no longer having to be horny, interesting and exciting 24x7. We divided the gold between us - Vivian declined a share, after all she was now an independently wealthy woman - and Beatrice and I parted as friends. As she pointed out, just before she packed her panties and left: "The two of us cannot afford not to be friends, Marius."